MORSELS

TALES OF LOVE AND PASSION

SERA MADDOX DRAKE

CONTENTS

INTRODUCTORY COMMENTS

Morsels is a collection of *eros*-themed short stories and micro-fiction. That does not mean all the stories contained within are works of erotica; only about half of what is in here would be defined as such, and only some of the more blatantly erotic stories are stand-alone. Two erotic short works in here are excerpts from my novel, *Ancilla*.

Eros is another word for love: passionate love, romantic love, desire.

Love is the subject of this anthology.

In "A Tale As Old As Time," we get to see, for a moment anyway, a hint of the growing love Beauty has for her Beast, and vice versa. Here I intimately explore what it means to be human. Are we determined by our bodies, or by our souls? What makes a man a man? Do our bodies determine the natures of our souls, or are we souls who happen to inhabit bodies? (Spoiler: It's the latter).

"A Rose By Any Other Name," another spicy cupcake of a story, shows what happens when two women come together for a very extreme first date after months and months of negotiation in a long-distance relationship. It has my ex-girlfriend's seal of approval.

"The Alpaca Yarn Incident" is a mildly spiced sex farce. When a medieval reen-actor's feast takes a turn for the "wurst," the narrator and her lovely lady exit the scene to hold a revel of their own. Since Monty Python's Flying Circus is involved, their two-person sewing circle becomes... *something completely different*. Bring out the comfy chair!

"One Of the Girls" shows what happens when an exotic dancer steals the name and sacred girdle of the Goddess of Love Herself.

The next two stories are concerned with love, as well, but they aren't light-hearted, and while they're erotic in nature, they're not comfortable. These are the only two stories in this volume that come with content advisories, and they're the equivalent of what in my youth used to be called "Very Special Episodes" in television sitcoms.

"Diving Into the Wreck" portrays what a formerly joyful BDSM relationship looks like when it has degenerated into abuse and misery – when the relationship is long over, but the two people in it can't admit that to themselves or to each other.

"Anything For a Friend," meanwhile, pairs BDSM with a love that is more philia than eros, and oh, by the way, the hero dies at the end of it. (That's not a spoiler. The end of the story is right there at the top of the page when you get to it).

Onward.

"Parliament of Rooks" is a homage to Geoffrey Chaucer and, to a much lesser degree, to Neil Gaiman (who was not a controversial figure at the time I wrote the story). It's a dream vision concerned with the origin of human love. If it doesn't seem to provide a satisfactory explanation for why people love the way they do, well, do keep in mind that this just-so story-within-a-story is told by a bird. How well do birds really understand people?

I've also included two chapters from *Ancilla*. If they whet your appetite, you are welcome to sate yourself on the main course that is available from Amazon and other online booksellers in both print and electronic form.

Many thanks to R.A. Volt, who provided feedback on my short stories and who has been a staunch supporter of mine ever since we exchanged our manuscripts (she read *Ancilla*, I read *The Whore* – which, for the record, is excellent). May our discussions of founding an intelligent smut movement spark beauty and delight.

A TALE AS OLD AS TIME

I'm lying in my curtained bed, resting. Sort of.

Really, I'm reading, and given the somewhat strenuous subject matter (Marlowe's *Doctor Faustus,* not translated into French) I can't really claim to be getting any rest, but this is supposed to be time spent on myself, used for napping or bathing or sitting on the window seat contemplating the garden outside, and I happen to be using it to get caught up on the rest of the reading list I brought with me when I came here, so I'm going to call it rest.

It isn't the first time I've broken the rules, and it probably won't be the last. So far, the invisible servants that manage this place have yet to report on my behaviour, and I have been very good about putting the books back where I've found them once I'm done reading them.

I want to read books to myself, in my room. It's not that I dislike having to read to him – this morning it was a treatise by Descartes – and I appreciate the necessity of keeping the books safe in the library, but I like being able to read on my own, in bed. At home I had very little time to spend on reading, and all my books got sold when my father sold off all the other possessions to pay off his bad debts, and I had to share the attic with my sisters once we moved to our new home, so I never had any space to myself any more than I had time to myself, after that, and reading books in a room that I can call my own, in a bed that I can curtain off from the world, seems like heaven.

He says he's not keeping me from taking books to my room out of jealousy, but out of a desire to keep the books safe. He says that. I'm not so sure. If my hands had been changed into wolf paws, with claws that shred paper when they try to turn pages, I'd be jealous of anyone who could hold a book properly to read it.

The bell chimes. Evening has been announced.

I put down Marlowe and slide my legs onto the footstool that has been provided to help me get in and out of bed. Once I am on the floor, the cold marble under my bare feet makes me shiver, but soon I'll bc in slippers.

Off with my chemise.

The invisible servants open the door of the wardrobe, and show me a selection of dresses. Red, green, black, yellow. The yellow dress is cut lower than I would ordinarily like, but I can always drape a shawl over my shoulders, and the roses embroidered on it in gold and silver and white thread are so lovely that I sigh with longing.

"That one." It has to be that one.

They choose slippers, petticoats, cage, and panniers for me, and a pale corset that lifts my miniscule breasts and actually makes it seem like I have a figure, then waft the dress over my body and tighten it in back. They do all this silently. If I hadn't been able to see the clothing moving out of the wardrobe, and if I hadn't heard them whispering at night when they thought I was asleep, I'd have thought my mind was playing tricks on me.

I don't know why their whispers somehow make them seem more real, less a product of mad delusion, but they do. I know the servants are real because they try to hide their voices from me.

Once I have been dressed, they direct me to the ballroom, lighting candles before me to indicate the way. By now, I could probably figure out the way on my own – I've been to the ballroom every night for the past two months – but having the candles lit for me is a courtesy. It is also, I suspect, a way to keep an eye on me, and to make sure that I don't try to leave the chateau without making my intentions known well in advance. I am allowed to leave, not that I would want to by the terms of the original agreement, but I cannot sneak away.

He is waiting for me. He is wearing the blue velvet coat and breeches that match his eyes, and go so well with his otherworldly silvery white fur. He's been dressed in this ensemble a few times before. I think he chooses it because he knows it takes my breath away.

"Shall we dance?" he asks, and extends a paw to me.

I gulp, and then nod. I have the right to refuse. I have not refused him yet. I don't think I have it in me to refuse him. "Yes," I reply, and walk toward him, and allow him to take me by the hand and circle my waist with one of his arms.

There will be no music played. It's not that sort of dancing we are about to do.

His breath is hot on my neck as he takes my flesh in his muzzle. Soft fur, sharp teeth. I gasp. He's not going to tear me apart and feast on me. He's not. He's never done it, and he won't do it. This has to be true. He's done far harsher things to me during the day, for his amusement, and he's always been able to hold himself in check. But his teeth are so sharp. They gnaw into me, and I bleed, and I shudder as his tongue laps at the blood trickling down my neck onto my back and chest.

He crushes me against him with his arm as he gets his taste of me. The cage under my dress does nothing to get in between me and his erection.

The dress is coming off, but it's already been ruined with my blood. Silk rips under his claws. The straps that hold the corset and cage on are next, and my torn clothing is flung to the side. My petticoats hang ridiculously from my hips. He pushes at them, snarls, and rends them. Blood on my thigh. He's raked me again. I still haven't healed from the last time he did that.

"Free me," he growls. I have to help him out of his breeches.

And then he is on me and in me and I cry out as he thrusts in deep and sinks his teeth in my chest and holds me down with his weight as I struggle. I can't help myself. I want him, but he is a *creature*, and my body rebels against this and fights this dance of ours every time we play it out. I kick, and I push with my legs and arms, and scream, and his only response is to seize my wrists in between his paws and pin my arms under his and take me harder.

It doesn't last long. He's too aroused by my struggles.

"*Ma belle cherie*," he murmurs, when he is spent. "Why must you fight me so?"

"I don't know." I really can't help myself. "I'm sorry."

"You're not finished yet, are you?"

"No."

"Of course not. I lost control too soon. Spread your legs."

I put my hands under my knees and spread myself apart for him, and he puts his head down and laps at me, working me with his tongue and furry muzzle until orgasm overtakes me and I convulse with pleasure and then lie on my back on the parquet floor, gasping, the mirrors and burning chandelier candles and the room itself spinning around me.

He has himself curled around me now, his arm draped over me possessively. I love it when he cuddles me like this. One winter when I was very little, there was a pack of wolves in the forest near our town, and I cried when my father joined the other hunters to exterminate the wolf pack; to me, they were not a threat, they were family, and I had dreamed of going into the woods and curling up next to them in the snow. It's silly, but I imagine the Beast curled against my body now feels like what the wolves of my childhood would have been, as companions.

I tense myself against what's going to come next.

"*Ma belle*, will you marry me?"

"No, Beast."

He always asks this. He knows I can't marry him.

But we can't let each other go.

The servants have cleaned up the shreds of my gown and underclothing, and left me a plain velvet dress to cover myself with. I pull it over my head and arms. I am past being embarrassed that they witness what goes on between me and my captor, but I draw the line at their helping me dress immediately after we have engaged in certain activities.

He's still wearing his velvet coat. I have to help him into his breeches, because he can't put them on himself, and there are no servants around to dress him. No one but me.

He's so beautiful in blue.

Later, we eat our dinner together. He likes the company. He must have been very lonely before my father stumbled into his garden, and they worked out the agreement that had me sent here as a hostage. I used to be repulsed by the Beast's dining habits, but his tearing into platefuls of raw meat no longer bothers me. It's not his fault he can't get his paws to hold a knife and fork properly, after all. He said he initially had his servants cut his meat up for him and feed him, but it just didn't feel right.

After dinner it will be time for me to retire to my bed and sleep. The servants will lead the way by lighting candles.

I'm starting to wish I didn't sleep in the great bed alone.

A Rose by Any Other Name

I have the lasagna in the oven, and a tossed salad of mixed spring greens, mint leaves, and pansies chilling in the refrigerator, also a cruet of blackberry-infused oil. It's a little early for blackberries, but fortunately I had some left in the freezer from last summer. A cheesecake made with three different kinds of chocolate waits on the shelf beneath. I've baked a decent, if not overpowering, mixture of ghost pepper sauce and sriracha sauce into it. It sounds weird, but it tastes rather good – you don't actually taste the pepper so much as feel it. It makes your mouth tingle and sting a little bit, and meanwhile, your taste buds get opened up so that you're more aware of the chocolate. A boiled artichoke sits on the counter, meanwhile, kept warm by a covering bowl, next to some lemon-and-garlic butter dipping sauce.

I don't believe in letting my guests go hungry.

"GRUNT: Pigorian Chant" plays on the CD player. I thought it would lighten things up a little while I cooked, while not actually being distracting later on. It sounds just like ordinary Gregorian chant unless you actually look at the lyric sheet – well, aside from the fact that the language used is pig Latin (what else?) Played low, you can't detect anything at all unusual in the chanting.

And now I'm putting the last touches on a foliage arrangement – long-stemmed roses, river birch branches, bamboo, all freshly harvested from my gardens, which are finally mature enough to use for cuttings. The cuttings go in a large urn, which I place on the dining table.

I have the house to myself for the weekend. That was a minor miracle, for which I am deeply grateful.

There is a knock at the door. I stop endlessly moving cuttings into new positions to answer it.

It's her, of course.

I take her overnight bag and make more busy work for myself by putting it in the hall closet for her, which takes all of a few seconds. I offer her chilled white wine. I load up the plates with food and put them on the table, which has already been set twice. I am a bundle of nerves and I am probably not good at hiding it. I hope that doesn't ruin things for her. Some people like the illusion of absolute self-assurance, and I have never been good at playing along with that. Acting is not my forte. With me, what you see is what you get.

Eating an artichoke properly is a rather involved process. The outside of the artichoke globe is very woody. You start by pulling off a leaf; then you dip the tender part into the butter, and you use your front teeth to strip the tender part of the artichoke leaf from the rest of it. As you work your way inward, the leaves gradually get tenderer until you get to the centre, the heart, which is soft enough to eat in its entirety without doing any stripping.

It can be an extremely sensuous experience.

Having finished our salads and our lasagna, we are down to the artichoke, and about halfway into it, I decide to start feeding her the leaves myself.

I tickle her lips gently with the soft end of an artichoke leaf before letting her nibble off the leaf end. Her lips are buttery. My fingers, too, are getting covered with butter, so after she is done swallowing her leaf, I give her my index finger to lick clean.

She smiles a little, and takes it into her mouth, sucking the butter off. Without being bidden, she does the same thing with my middle finger, then my ring finger, before finally licking the butter off where it has begun to dribble down my wrist.

That's good.

I swallow a large ball of nerves – they threaten to stick in my throat and choke me, but they go down – and bend toward her to sample her lips. They are soft and warm, and taste of flavoured butter, which is delightful, so I start slowly licking off the butter, occasionally biting down to see how she responds. Soft moans. Soft gasps. I move in and circle around her tongue, exploring. She is shaking now. I'll take that.

"This is delicious," I say, "but it distracts from dessert."

"What's dessert?" she asks.

"You."

Her, accompanied by a few other ingredients, to be more specific.

I stand up and take the black silk scarf out of my apron pocket, the scarf I've designated as the blindfold for the evening. It's probably more melodramatic than it needs to be, which is a point in its favour. No, we're not going very far, the living room is right by the dining room table – there isn't enough room to swing a cat in the bedroom, let alone anything else – but a few steps of blindness can be very interesting, and besides, she looks cute blindfolded.

"I need your body to be disrobed. Strip," I murmur, and she gets about halfway done taking off her blouse and skirt before I start to help her anyway, because fumbling with buttons and bra straps gives me an excuse to fumble with a few other things. Oh, well.

I managed to get the ropes around both her and the couch in a more or less acceptable manner. The resulting arrangement is more serviceable than aesthetic, because I've never been good with knots and the whole thing is a bit of a jury-rig, really, but that's another advantage to blindfolding people: they don't have to see your unattractive rope arrangements. I had somebody make suggestions on how to improve my ropes once, and proceed to help me get them put in a better system of knots. That was embarrassing. It didn't completely kill the mood, but still…

Speaking of embarrassing, I quickly double-check to make sure I did indeed remember to close all the blinds. There are some things the neighbors really don't need to see.

The arrangement I have set up right now leaves her entire backside exposed from head to toe. It also leaves her head free. My ball gag went missing. I'm hoping it doesn't turn up somewhere truly awkward, like the children's toy bin in the kitchen. This had better not get too noisy.

I did remember to put down dark flat sheets on the couch and on the floor as drop cloths, though.

"How do you feel about flower arrangements?" I ask.

"*What?*"

"Because you get to help me deconstruct a flower arrangement I made a short while ago. I think you saw it on the table when we sat down to eat. Which part of the arrangement would you like to help me remove first? The roses, the birch branches, or the bamboo stalks?"

She gasps a little. "Oh. You..."

"It all has to come down."

"All of it?"

"All of it."

That was a hiss. I think she just hissed at me. In fact, I'm sure of it.

"Birches. I guess... It's all going to be evil, isn't it?"

I smile. Wait, she can't see that. "Pretty much," I reply. "The birch branches are probably the lesser of evils, though."

"Fine. Birches."

I decide to be nice and use up all the birches right away, and not hard enough to do much more than redden the skin and make a dramatic and scary swishing noise followed by a nice, satisfying thwack. Besides, I don't want to use up my energy on the birches when I'll need it for the other foliage.

Things have become a bit messy. After I used up the birch branches, she couldn't decide which implement of destruction to get out of the way next, so we wound up flipping a coin, and bamboo won. It could have been worse – I could have soaked the bamboo stalks in the bathtub before arranging them, rather than just letting them get a little wet from the water in the urn, but bamboo is still bamboo, and there were eight stalks, so I wound up making a lot of welts up and down her back and legs.

My arm is a bit tired. I'm resting it as I sponge her down.

There is a particularly large welt on her upper left buttock; I kiss it and work at it with my tongue before applying the sponge. The response I get is gratifyingly expressive. She moans very prettily.

I haven't heard her scream yet.

"That feels wonderful," she sighs, as the warm sponge gently drips water onto her skin.

"It won't in a minute," I reply. "What, you think I'm moistening your skin just because I want to be nice?"

That wasn't a very polite word she just called me.

I sigh and get my cowhide gauntlets. I'm going to need them. This particular strain of heirloom rose, a climber that likes to reproduce itself aggressively, necessitating frequent pruning, is particularly thorny, especially on the young branches.

"There are six rose branches. I think I'll use them one at a time. They still have their roses on – nicely fragranced, aren't they? – although I doubt that will last for long. Say when."

She doesn't say "when," so much as hisses it, or maybe spits it. Never mind. It's still a "when."

I pick up the first rose branch and lash out at her back with all my might.

She actually managed to get through three of the rose branches before safe-wording, which surprised the hell out of me. I had only expected her to endure one or two blows.

The messiness quotient has increased exponentially. Her back is covered with blood. There is blood on her buttocks and on her legs; there is blood on the drop cloths. There is a little bit of blood on the walls. I'll have to research effective cleaning methods tonight. No, I've never exactly dealt with this problem before.

She's gasping for air. "I need to bite down on something," she pants, "unless you want me to scream at the top of my lungs."

This wasn't a stop, it was a temporary pause? Oh, my stars... I have to kiss her, now. I move around the couch, take her face in my hands, and devour her until she moans, her body writhing against the couch and the ropes.

Ouch.

"No, not me," I snap. "Now how is that going to accomplish anything?"

She chuckles.

"Besides, I need my hands free." A really nasty idea whispers to me. I judge it acceptable. "I have two more rose branches to break on your back."

"Two?"

She's doing the math.

I take one of the remaining rose branches and put it in her mouth. "You did say you needed to bite down on something. You might not want to bite down too hard, though."

It's about to get a little noisy, I think.

She did indeed scream. She let the rose branch drop from her mouth when she did it; fancy that. I decided to not re-use the branch, and stuck to using the two rose branches that remained in the urn. I did say I was only going to use two more, and I don't believe in going back on my word. It didn't take very long for the branches to snap, either, although I imagine it felt a lot longer to be on the receiving end than it actually took.

The living room is an utter mess.

She is beautifully, magnificently bloody. I busy myself licking her clean now that I've got her out of the ropes and crumpled on the couch. I'll have to wash her and put actual antiseptic and dressings on afterward, of course, but there is no way I'm going to let the blood go to waste, and she doesn't seem inclined to stop me from feasting on it.

It's sweet, like tangerines, tangerines in a copper bowl.

Intoxicated by her ragged gasps and the taste of her blood, I reach out, grab her face in my hands, and devour her mouth. Sweetness. Moaning. Rocking. She wraps her arms around me, thrusting her tongue into my mouth. It's too much for me; I let my hand slide down to her breast, finding her nipple, massaging it slowly and methodically. Louder moaning.

"If you're not going into shock," I whisper, "I think I'll have you, now."

"No," she replies, hoarsely. "I mean, no, I'm not in shock. I want... I want..."

"It's all right. I get the idea."

I slide further down the couch. There are other parts of her that I think need devouring.

Lying next to her in the curtained bed. Eating chocolate hot pepper cheese-cake. Drinking limeade to replace lost fluids. Wearing loose nightgowns – she, to provide an extra layer of protection for her bloody welts and keep them from getting scraped by the bed sheets, I because I don't generally sleep in the nude. I've never been fond of the way it feels. I like nude cuddling, but not nude sleeping. No, I have no idea why that is.

"This," she says, "is incredible cheesecake."

I smile. "Thank you. I thought about you almost nonstop while preparing dinner. I really did want to make things you'd like."

"Mmm. Did you enjoy it, yourself?" A wicked smile plays across her face as she reaches across and finds the wet spot between my legs that I'd more or less been trying to ignore for the duration of the evening's activities, making me gasp with shock, then whimper. "I think you did…"

It's going to be a very long night.

THE ALPACA YARN
INCIDENT

There is an extremely cute lady in a cotehardie at this reenactors' feast, and she seems to be flirting with me. I think. I'm not sure. It could just be my wishful thinking, and, alas, wishful thinking on the part of the lustful does not constitute flirtation on the part of the object of lust.

"If we were Vikings, we could marry very easily," she says, all glancing, laughing eyes. "All I'd need to do would be to say, 'I marry you! I marry you! I marry you!' in public, and then we'd be married."

"I thought that was Bedouins."

"It might be Berbers..." She pauses to think for a moment. "Anyway, we're in public, so now we're married."

"But what if I don't want to be married to someone I just met?"

"Oh. Well. Divorce is easy, too."

Fair enough.

We're sitting below the salt; the food is a little more basic than that served near the high table, but there's plenty of it. There is also plenty of mead going around, because we're sitting next to a friend of hers who is a mead maker, and unsurprisingly, this section of the dining area is a crowded and popular one, despite there being fewer removes of food. The apple melomel being passed around the table right now is particularly nice. I don't like the out of control feeling that being drunk gives me, but I'm starting to notice a bit of a buzz, because the meads have all been too delicious to pass up. I decide to just get smaller samples from now on, so that I stay more or less sober but don't have to miss out on the mead tasting.

The next remove (for us) is a hearty stew made from beef, parsnips, carrots, leeks, mushrooms, and red wine, simmered with juniper berries. It needs just a little more seasoning, in my opinion, so I add coarse sea salt and ground black pepper from the little cellars I've put on the table with the rest of my feast gear and offer them to the lady who has been keeping me company. Cinnamon, I think; what this stew needs is a tiny pinch of cinnamon to bring out the savory character of the meat. Cassia would also work. The two spices are not the same, although they are similar enough in flavor that people frequently confuse them. (Cassia is more pungent than cinnamon).

"Much better than the soup," she says as she digs in, and I have to agree with her, although just about anything would be an improvement over the soup, the prime ingredient of which was apparently burnt, grated sandalwood, which made the soup smell unsettlingly like rotting leeches. Probably the taste was similar, although I have never ingested rotten leeches, nor did I bring myself to sample the soup.

As we are finishing our bowls of stew, the next performer is announced: a bard who is well known for his off-key singing, strained versification – when he butchers the work of others, the effect is bad enough, but he even manages to butcher his own work, and the end result is even worse – and, in mundane life, equally well known for his fondness for Rush Limbaugh. He wears a purple houpelande, purple hat, purple boots, and, according to rumor, a number of other purple things that are intimate enough that I prefer not to imagine them, at least not on him. "There probably won't be much dancing tonight," she says, pouting a little. "It's already seven, feast hasn't ended, and we still have to have court. And you know how windy this king likes to get."

Unfortunately, I do. He has all the thespian ambition of the last monarch, with none of the actual acting presence.

"Wasn't somebody supposed to get knighted tonight?"

"Not that I'm aware of. However, I filled out more than a hundred award-of-arms scrolls as a scribal volunteer today."

A bad bard, a long and boring royal court, no dancing. No wonder our table companions seem eager to drink all the mead that's available for sampling. I feel sorry for the designated drivers, who will have to endure the evening's events without the benefit of self-medication. "Post-revel?"

"Won't start early. Want to hang out at my place until it gets off the ground?"

The bard starts singing. I shudder. There are times that I hate being sensitive to pitch.

"Yes, please..."

I'm sitting on the couch, surrounded by balls of yarn and half-completed sewing projects, and if I'm extremely careful, I don't need to see the pins holding the fabric of the uncompleted garb together. My lady companion is on the floor cutting fabric to a surcoat pattern. We've been doing this for a couple of hours, now, while watching recorded episodes of Monty Python's Flying Circus. An unusual way to spend a wedding night, but then, we did only just meet each other.

She didn't ask me to carry her over the threshold, for which I am grateful. I'm fairly strong, or so I've been told, but I didn't want to put it to the test, at least not until after the effects of the mead tasting wore off.

They're climbing the north face of Uxbury Road as I wind alpaca yarn around my fingers, in preparation for making a pompom. I've been making pompoms. I've been filling a wicker basket with pompoms. This is my last pompom; after I tie it off and trim it, I toss it into the basket with the others and pick up another skein of yarn, of a particularly soft and fuzzy variety. It's dyed a lovely shade of heathery violet. This, in turn, almost threatens to make me think of the purple-clad bard we fled the feast hall to escape – no, no, I really don't want to let my mind go there. This has been a pleasant day so far.

"What is this stuff?" I ask, making a loop and tying it around my left index finger. "It's positively decadent."

"Alpaca," she replies.

"Ah."

From the video, something about storage jars. I begin weaving the yarn into a rope, using my fingers as a loom.

Minutes go by. I weave. She cuts and pins. Bouzouki music plays. There is no cheese.

"Are you ever going to make a move on me?" she asks.

"Um. I didn't know you fancied me."

"I married you, didn't I? Good grief, what more do you want?"

I can think of a few things. I bend down and kiss her neck, planting kisses on her until she leans back and meets her mouth with mine. Her hair is a cloud of brown curls, tickling my cheek, and I bury my fingers in it. There is a subtle scent of spice in the air.

"Cloves," I murmur, "you smell like cloves..."

"It's my shampoo. I get it from a soap maker I know."

We spend more time exploring each other. Under the cotehardie is lovely, soft warmth. She moans nicely.

I fumble.

I can't figure out how to remove her clothing.

"Could you please take off the cotehardie?" I whisper. "Also. Would you please shut that bloody bouzouki music up? It's distracting."

She giggles as she complies.

No more bouzouki music. No more clothing. Much better.

And now for something completely different.

"Could you hold this for me, please?"

She gives me a puzzled look, but holds out her hands for the ball of yarn that I put in them. It is still attached to about three feet of finger-knitting, which I detach with her sewing scissors and tie off before I wrap it around her wrists.

"Well," she says with a smile, "I wasn't expecting that."

"No one does. So. I presume you have a comfy chair."

Yes, of course I had to say it.

Having ascertained that the recent twist in the evening's events was not unwelcome, and firmly settled her in the comfy chair with the help of more yarn, I get back to the business of interrogating her. She might, after all, be a dangerous heretic. So far, I haven't detected any suspicious witch's marks on her mouth, her ears, her breasts, or her thighs, although there's always a possibility of missing something important, so I double-check and triple-check my work for errors. No, no marks. A certain amount of moisture, but I don't think it has anything to do with witchcraft or heresy.

Of course, I haven't brought out the soft cushions yet. There may still be a confession.

"*Aufputzen*," I say, reaching into the wicker basket.

"*Gesundheit*," she replies.

I shake my head. Should have seen that one coming. "Pompoms. They're German pompoms. German hunters used them to quiet their bowstrings." There. That's a nicely sized one. Like the others, it has long strings attached, to make it easier to tie it on to a crossbow. I tickle her with the pompom, eliciting a gratifyingly loud gasp. "Interestingly enough, the word *Aufputzen* is remarkably similar to the word *Aufputschen*, which is German for stimulant." In goes the yarn ball. "Rather bizarre that the word for something that silences something is almost identical to the word for stimulant, isn't it?"

"Er. Um..."

Hot, ragged moans.

"Well? Do you confess?"

"I'm – I'm not – I don't understand what I'm accused of!"

Clearly she is made of harder stuff.

I start to work on her with my tongue. We'll see if that gets a confession out her – or at least a lot of shouting.

No heresy in this apartment. Also, no false grail beacons and no larches, which is probably just as well, all things considered.

We cuddle together, naked, weak-kneed, and exhausted. Interrogation can be so tiring.

It also tends to make me hungry.

"Do you have any cheese?" I ask.

She hits me in the head with a pillow.

ONE OF THE GIRLS

The music throbbed and groaned; it begged for release, but no end was in sight. Just when it looked like the day might finally reach a climax and there would be some rest, somebody came in through the door five dollars lighter than they'd been previously; and it was time to put another dollar in the jukebox and get up on stage again. No rest for the wicked, no end in sight.

The day had been a busy one. One of the newer girls, Wildfire (and no, she did not fit her name, aside from the red hair – she ought to have picked something sensible like Sheila or Kelly) seemed to have picked up a regular clientele, and she was making a fortune. Without turning tricks, no less. Only four hours into her shift and she'd already amassed a little over six hundred dollars.

At one of the bigger bars, like the Mustang, you could see it – but here, in the Red Garter? Unheard of! The Red Garter was one of those cheap downtown sleaze buckets that basically offered little more than a warm spot for the street-walkers to hang their coats and sit for a while. More tricks got turned out of that kind of bar than went on in a David Copperfield show. The owners were too cheap to pay off the police, so the bar and the adjoining bookstore got raided by the vice squad about once per month. If the owners had paid any taxes on the Red Garter at all, it must have been a write-off, because the bar never made any money. When a place is closed down regularly for health violations or solicitation, how could it be possible to make money pulling in horny businessmen off the street? If they came to this place at all, they came after they got their fifty-dollar box lunches at the Mustang, which were served to them by topless waitresses; they came after they tipped Bunny Glamazon (68GGG – 22 – 38) two hundred and fifty bucks; they came to try and spend their remaining twenty dollars on a quick private show and some efficient chimpanzee spanking. If they came at all.

But here was Wildfire pulling in the bucks. A week ago, she wasn't making jack. But now...Miss Shake-Your-Little-Money-Maker, in the flesh.

She liked to claim that it was all in the garter she wore: a little gold thing, looked like it was sewn together out of doubloons and jewels, straight from the set of Treasure Island. Quite tacky. It would have gone great with some Las Vegas ostrich feathers and a matching gold collar, but showgirl plumes would have scraped the low ceiling, especially since Wildfire tended to wear six-inch stilettos. In gold. At least those matched. Her outfits generally didn't – they varied from a black business suit to a Victorian corset – but since the Red Garter was a nude bar, it didn't matter; they'd come off anyway.

An hour later, and she'd grossed a thousand. Five-o-clock rush. Where was she getting it from?

After a month of this money-making, the Red Garter decided to make Wildfire the Girl Of The Week in the local dribble sheets. When they brought the photographer in, she smiled. "I've got a new name," she said.

About time!

"Oh, yeah? What is it, pretty lady?"

"Aphrodite."

"It'll never work. Guys don't like names with more than two syllables. Takes too much thought."

"They'll remember me."

"Oh, yeah?"

"Yeah. Just watch. You'll see."

New girls are always needed in this profession. No matter how good you are, how much they love you, the management always finds an excuse to fire you. They say it's because you're too fat, too thin, too flat, too big-busted, too tall, too short, or too obvious about being a hooker; but the real reason is that the managers get bored of you and want you to make your money somewhere else. If any girl lasts longer than a few months, she's probably between the sheets with one of the owners.

At about three o'clock on a Tuesday afternoon, during the slowest part of the day, a new girl knocked on the door of the Red Garter. She had a boy with her, very pretty – too pretty to be her boyfriend, so he had to be her pimp. She wanted an audition. Whatever. Why not. They let her in.

When she got up onto the stage, she was not the best dancer in the world – but she had beautiful long golden-blonde hair that went nearly down to her knees; and eyes to match. She was gold and white and rosy and very, very curvy in all the right places. She could have been a porn star, with that body. People have sketched bodies like that and used the curves to construct the perfect blow-up doll. Most importantly of all, though, her hair was natural, and so were her various feminine parts.

She got hired.

"What name do you want?" the manager asked her.

"Aphrodite," she said with a heart-wrenching smile.

"Sorry. It's been taken."

She frowned. A look of confusion glided across her face.

"Taken?"

"By one of the other dancers. You'll have to pick a new one."

"I will settle for Peleia, perhaps."

The manager rolled his eyes. "Oh God. Not another girl with a thing for weird names. How do you spell that?"

One night Aphrodite (nee Wildfire) got approached backstage by the new dancer, who wanted to know the secret of her dancing.

"You pick it up after a few days. After a month or two you'll be really good. Just watch what the other girls do, and do it. Do you like girls?"

"I beg your pardon?"

"That's a lovely accent you have. Italian? Strange, you don't look Italian. Right. Anyway. It helps if you have some lesbian tendencies, because then you can pick up the moves that turn you on. What turns you on might turn on the customers, and that gives you a bit of an advantage. Otherwise, just watch for what looks kind of neat, and watch the way the men react to it." The song stopped. "Time for me to go on. See 'ya."

She ran out of the cramped dressing room – which wasn't really a dressing room at all, just a large closet that had been converted into a women's bathroom and given a few milk crates in the back to store bags of costumes – and started her set. The sounds of Madonna's "Like a Virgin" filled the air (because today she was wearing a bridal veil and a white dress with her gold shoes and garter). But halfway through the song, the music stopped. Jukebox failure? And where did the lights go? Was it already time for another power failure? When was the fuse box going to get replaced?...

A golden fire, as if from some fierce sun, seemed to emanate from the dressing room. The door slammed open, and a bright light silhouetted the figure of a goddess. For once, Aphrodite (who was once Wildfire) got no attention.

"You have stolen my girdle, and now you steal my *name?*" the figure called out. Her voice, unlike the nimbus surrounding her, was cold. "I command you to return them."

When a goddess commands you, you don't argue with her. Seconds elapsed. Nobody breathed. Then Aphrodite was gone in a puff of dawn-vapor and scent, leaving Wildfire (now Wildfire) naked on the dance floor.

The men tipped her well, out of sympathy.

Two weeks later, there was another opening at the Red Garter, since Wildfire had been fired for being "too much." A round girl appeared. She danced well, if a bit self-consciously. She was hired. When the management heard about her taking a job as a dancer so that she could catch her husband in the act of cheating on her, they had a good laugh.

"So what's your dance name going to be?" they asked.

"Hera."

Those girls. Couldn't they ever pick something normal?

THE MUSE

I'm working again on a new one, a study of the female nude (okay, so I'm going through a nude phase - at least it isn't a still-life-with-soup-can phase, because soup cans were overdone from the first moment Andy Warhol decided to make them art). This nude is not from a real model, but from a Rodin sculpture. Or a series of them. There's a mermaid that I particularly like; also the woman in "The Kiss," and, for sheer dramatic effect, the fallen caryatid. I like Rodin's work. It's incredibly expressive. I wonder what made him burn.

This one should be good. Her skin I'm coloring ivory - alabaster white - because most of Rodin's sculptures were carved from white marble. The only color I allow the woman in my painting is in her hair. I paint it red. The hair on her head becomes piles and piles of flame, like an autumn bonfire, while the hair on her pubis gets painted the dark, brownish red of dried blood. Red is for passion, and Rodin would, I think, have liked me to do this tribute to his work in all these various shades of red.

She's turning out beautiful. Radiant. My angel of fire.

I think I will call the subject of my paintings Venus. It seems only appropriate.

I've painted a whole series of her now. Some of the studies have been done in the classical tradition, including a "Venus Pudica" based on Botticelli's, only her hair isn't covering her - it's billowing completely out to sea, to the glowing orange-rose sunrise. I can't seem to stop, which is great. When the inspiration hits you, you should milk it until every last drop is wrung from its source.

I *have* remembered to eat, although I don't feel like sleeping. I have a pot of cappuccino by my elbow, and a plate of prawn and lemon sandwiches. I'm sensible. I'm not one of those artists who never takes care of her body. I'm also not so poor that I'll literally starve in a garret. Things sometimes get a little tight, of course - now, for instance - but that's not the same thing as destitution.

It's really strange, but every time I look at my original Venus, a shudder runs through me, and I have to paint again. It's almost uncanny. Can a painting you've made yourself also be your muse?

I pour myself another cup of cappuccino and draw a sketch for my next effort, which (I have decided this with my usual humour) shall be of Pygmalion and Galatea. A triptych; in scene three, Galatea will be seen coming to life and giving her hand to her sculptor. She will, of course, have flame-coloured hair, like the subject I am basing her on.

I am proud of my efforts. I do not think I will market these - I couldn't bear to have them sold. I tell myself (or try to tell myself, anyway) that this is because my nudes are too experimental. But I think the real reason is that I'm in love with them. It's fairly common for an artist to fall in love with her own work, I've heard. I remember reading that somewhere. Usually, we get over it. I suppose, in a few months, I'll get sick of all this clutter in my study, and then I'll try to pawn it off on Frevd or some other hip coffeehouse or arty wine bar. Whether they'll take it or not is another story. I hope they do, because I could use the money. My last client still hasn't paid me off completely for the paintings I gave her as office decorations. Maybe I should get a day job.

But then, how could I finish this series? I can't work when a job keeps interrupting my flow, I've tried that -

Best to not think about it. Best to just work on my Venus.

A miracle! Not only did my client finally pay me, but she gave me a bonus and may know of a friend who would be willing to buy and exhibit some of my work! That takes care of the bills for the next two or three months, anyway.

The Pygmalion-Galatea triptych is finished, and (I must be going mad) my Venus is looking at me with what seems to be an approving eye.

Even more mad, I am in love. This is not just infatuation. It is *love*. I know this. I can't resist my desires any longer. Kissing the oily feet of my Venus seems beautiful, voluptuous; holy. It is the only right thing to do.

I surrender.

I found out where yesterday's manic delirium came from. It seems I have flu. It's horrible. I have a fever of (since the last time I checked, which was an hour ago) nearly a hundred and five degrees. Something tells me I really should call the doctor, but I can't get out of bed. The sheets are soaked. I feel as though I'm rotting; my body is an empty shell. I can't imagine how much strength it would take for me to reach the phone, which is in the next room, of course.

My Venus stares down at me from where she is positioned in my loft - my daybed is right next to my work area. It makes the paints more accessible when I wake up in the morning. My Venus is concerned. Her lips move, slow and blurry. Mostly, I can't really make out what she is saying, but if I listen really closely, I do catch some of it. "Poor Alice!" she says (Alice being my name - goddesses always seem to know your name). "I fear I'll be the death of you!"

I try to reassure her, to remind her that dying for one's art is actually a sweet and traditional thing to do - it even ensures one's fame a few generations down the road - but she shakes her head sadly. She doesn't want me to die. She wants me alive.

She wants to know if I love her.

Of course, I love you, I respond. *Don't we all worship the source of our inspiration?*

She wants to come down, even though the results are often fatal. I let her.

Will you make me some chicken soup? I ask. *And find my acetaminophen?*

Well, it is a dream, after all.

"Of course," she says, reassuring me. She'll do anything to make my service more comfortable.

I smile weakly and sink into oblivion. My next painting - oh, it will have to be a tribute to Bosch or Dali. What a strange Venus will rise out of this fever, if I ever get up from it.

It's been a few days. I feel weak and drained, but at least my fever is gone. For some strange reason, I've got bruises all over me, especially on my thighs and neck - I must have fallen out of bed and walked into the door, or something. Maybe it's just a weird side effect of this horrid flu. I still have a lingering cough. But there's a package of ibuprofen and some cough medicine by the bed, and some honey and lemon juice and a bottle of whiskey, which added to hot water are my usual cure-all. A hot toddy won't actually cure you of your ills, but it will distract you enough that you stop caring how rotten you feel.

I begin to paint my dream-illustration series, which I decided should be a collection of egg tempura miniatures painted on ten-centimeter blocks of wood.

I've been having the strangest dreams now, strange even for me. Most involve my Venus coming down and asking me to put a little more blood into my paintings. As if she were a woman who stepped out of the mind of Edvard Munch, she likes blood. And, she says, it gives the paintings *such* a delightfully rich color.

I've tried it. Crazy, but wouldn't you know, she's right. It mixes beautifully with the egg tempera. My miniatures glow, icons of an earlier pagan faith. The gold leaf gleams when the sun shines on them through the skylight. It's been doing that a lot, lately, at least in the mornings - and as beautiful as the effect is, it hurts my eyes. I worry that it will fade the paint, too, so I decide to keep my paintings covered except at night. I'm starting to work primarily at night now, anyway.

The coloring in my paintings is changing. It's getting richer and more sensuous.

I am exhausted. Totally, and utterly, exhausted. I cannot paint anymore, no matter how demanding my muse is. I need a rest. My cough is coming back, and I always seem to have a horrible chill.

I bruise easily, and constantly. The bruises appear all over my body, in strange locations, like my inner thighs, and never seem to heal. I don't remember how I got them. I'm afraid to call the doctor for fear of finding out something horrible about myself.

My Venus, my muse, whispers to me from the painting, promising to finally manifest herself - wouldn't I like a more three-dimensional model, when I recover?

Certainly, I tell her. If only she'll be patient and let me sleep for a few more days.

She smiles and grants my wish.

I am rocked (I'm too tired to come up with anything original) in the arms of oblivion.

It's sundown. I don't know how long I've slept. My muse is in the kitchen area, fixing me clam linguini - because, she says, I need my carbohydrates. An empty bottle of Aqua Vitae lies drained by my bedside table. I think I guzzled it in five seconds flat.

There's a bruise on my left breast. My muse put it there. Quite an impressive hickey, really. I still call her Venus because she hasn't given me any other name to call her yet.

She comes to my bed, props me up on pillows, and feeds me, telling me stories - mostly from Ovid. I think she may be reciting from memory, but I'm not the proper scholar to be a judge of that. She has a beautiful voice, and her touch is both soothing and wildly arousing. She is very kind.

I have a whole slew of ideas on how to paint her, already. I look forward to it.

I am so glad to have got her attention.

As for the bruises, the exhaustion - well, they mean nothing to me. So she has a fetish. It's a small price to pay for the favors of a muse.

DIVING INTO THE WRECK

I wrote this after cobbling together some old scribblings that I'd written when I was in a love affair that had gone south. It's a story about what BDSM relationships look like after they've soured past the point of no return.

(That's something we don't talk about in the scene, you know: Sometimes things go badly wrong. It's not just vanilla, heteronormative couples that develop problems, growing abuse cycles like cancerous growth. Kinked people can have miserable relationships too. Kinked people can get abusive to each other. It's not all safe, sane, consensual utopia for us. We're human. Like all human beings, we are imperfect. Like all human beings, we can hurt each other in bad ways, ways we never bargained for).

Trying to show lovemaking after the love had more or less gone, trying to depict sex that was desired but only with growing amounts of ambivalence, and trying to write about kink that had spoiled as badly as the vanilla aspects of the sex had was an interesting challenge. I wanted to write something that was not romanticized sexual assault but was not joyful by any stretch of the imagination, either. I wanted to show two people who were in pain, and who were lying to themselves and each other about the health of their relationship.

It was a fine tightrope that I walked, and I did it all for the sake of showing off a couple of characters who I hope the reader agrees with me should have broken up with each other ages ago.

If anyone reading it finds elements of the story arousing, but it's the most damned uncomfortable sort of arousal possible, good. *That means I succeeded in capturing the miserable ambivalence of what it feels like to be in the late stages of an unhealthy relationship that is in its death throes.*

Because here's the thing about abuse: It starts slowly, almost undetectable. The red flags are so small, and they don't wave much. Eventually, once things have degenerated, love begins to turn to hate, and it hurts because hate is not the opposite of love - it's love gone to rot.

The opposite of love is not hate. It's indifference.

The worst part of abuse is that the only way to end it is to leave. Caught early on, couples therapy might mend things, but the vast majority of abusers don't want to change anything about themselves, thus, don't want to change the relationship.

The worst flashbacks and dreams are not the bad memories, either. They're the happy ones. You will be forever haunted by what could have been.

I triggered myself while writing this.

Speaking of triggers, here are some trigger warnings: Implied domestic and financial abuse. Miserable sex that I won't dignify by calling it "lovemaking," although I'm sure the characters in the story would. Impact play, bondage, power exchange, and above all, sorrow.

I came to explore the wreck.
The words are purposes.
The words are maps.
I came to see the damage that was done
and the treasures that prevail.
ADRIENNE RICH

She watched him look about the room in dismay.

"You still haven't done the dishes. The litter boxes haven't been cleaned in two days. There are dust bunnies the size of antelopes on the stairs. You haven't sorted your mail in two weeks - and your idea of straightening up is to move the unsorted piles of paper from one part of the house to another. You haven't put away the laundry..."

He is at least right about that, she thought.

She was a terrible housekeeper and always had been. Her style of cleaning and tidying was to put all chores off until the weekend, then try to tackle everything in one fell swoop, usually only succeeding in getting around to half the chores on her to-do list.

Gesturing at the highest pile of clothes, which was probably the clean laundry, he bellowed, *"Do I have to do everything around here?"*

Oh, no. Not that old argument. Not on Valentine's Day.

She hadn't been able to get him the flowers she'd wanted, because there were no bouquets of long-stemmed roses on sale for less than fifty dollars. No romantic dinner of "Marry-Me Beef Stroganoff," because she was a lousy cook. No wine. No *Romeo and Juliet* performance. No money.

She hated herself for not being able to hold down the sort of job that paid enough to give them all the things they wanted, or failing that, a gesture at the conventional trappings of romance. These arguments about her failings as a housekeeper only served to remind her of another area in which she would be deficient. The timing couldn't have been worse.

Then again, they'd never managed to have a good Valentine's Day.

Last year, their girlfriend broke up with them, saying she felt like a unicorn they were trying to put in a stable and ride on whenever they needed to forget their relationship problems.

The year before that, she'd been living in Glasgow, and he'd decided to fly over to surprise her, which would have been fantastic, except she'd already made plans with her other boyfriend, who was local to the area and thus far more likely to be available on Valentine's Day than he, and the resulting diplomatic kerfuffle climaxed with the Scottish boyfriend quite understandably having a complete meltdown. Romantic, what?

And before *that* was their first Valentine's Day together as a couple. Their first Valentine's Day, their first six-month anniversary, their first month together in their very first apartment. That time they'd had enough money to buy long-stemmed roses, with which they'd planned to beat each other, but both of them had terrible fevers due to flu, so the kinkfest they'd dreamed of never happened. That night, all the SM consisted of Sneezing and Moaning.

This year's Valentine's Day didn't seem to be looking any better.

"Enough," he said, and grabbed her hand.

And so she found herself dragged behind him as he led her down the stairs into the basement.

"The washing machine won't bite you. It's me you should worry about, not the washing machine."

She didn't like the basement in their building. She didn't like basements, period. They were chilly, moldy, damp places, full of dark corners and scary. No matter how well-lit the basement was, how organized and tidy, it was still a basement. She only liked basements to be used for one purpose: hiding from tornados.

The washing machine stood against the west wall of the basement, solid and stubborn. Equally solid and stubborn was the load of laundry that sat in front of it. She'd managed to get one load done that day: a load of white socks that she hadn't yet dried.

He sighed when he opened the washing machine door.

"Put those in the dryer."

"I don't take orders. I'm not a waitress."

"Really? Fine, then. I'll do it. I do everything else." He threw heaps of socks from the washer into the dryer, tossed in a dryer sheet, and hit the button that would start them baking. He then put his arms into the heap of dirty laundry on the floor, shoveled clothes into the washer along with a couple of detergent pods, and checked the settings on the washer. "At least this way I can set the temperature myself. This is the last time you ever wash my dark shirts in hot water and dry everything for seventy minutes."

"Do we have to start that again?"

"Yes. Hopefully, it won't become a habit."

She sensed a row coming on.

This time, however, instead of launching into the usual argument, he grabbed her by the waist. She didn't even have time to protest before she found herself tossed over the washing machine.

Her body landed on the lid with a loud *whump*.

She found her hands pinned behind her back. Within seconds, the Velcro restraints were on her wrists, and her sweatpants were on the floor. Her athletic shirt stayed where it was since he couldn't take it off around the restraints. Then came the blindfold.

Usually, their arguments were of the nasty, spoken, acidic kind. This was new. This was just plain weird.

"You realize," she said, "that anyone can see into the basement? The lights are on. It's lighter in here than it is out there. We're in full view."

"So we are. You've been a stripper, haven't you? Why the modesty? I'm not ashamed of what I'm about to do. I'm not ashamed of *us*. Are you?"

She was so busy mulling that over that she barely noticed when he shackled her ankles. She did notice when he gagged her, though, because she hated gags. At least it wasn't a ball gag. Those were the worst. She had a hard time breathing around ball gags, even the small ones. They made her choke on her mucus until she felt like she was drowning. They made her wheeze. It wasn't asthma, exactly. She wasn't sure what it was. She just knew she didn't deal well with gags.

"That," he said, "is so the people upstairs can't hear your screams through the heating vents."

Oh, like they can't hear whatever else comes from the basement?

She chuckled softly to herself. This seemed an absurd way to solve their problems.

"Chuckle all you want. You won't be doing it before long."

That was all the warning she got.

The paddle laid into her hard and fast. Dammit. She hated that thing. It wasn't a sex toy; it was a fucking meat tenderizer. She'd threatened to whale on him with it one day, the same way he used it to beat her buttocks into a solid mass of bruises. She didn't think he'd enjoy it, though, which meant he would be unlikely to put up with the abuse long enough to sustain that kind of bruising. Unlike her, he wasn't one to grit his teeth and put up with activities or people that he hated. His pride was a different sort of pride from hers.

Despite her best efforts to cut off her perve wiring, her body responded. She wriggled against the washing machine. She wasn't sure whether she wanted to relieve her tension or just escape the paddle. It wasn't much of a success, either way. She was too well restrained.

She felt his fingers teasing her between her legs, sliding deep into somewhere wet and slithery.

"You're enjoying this."

My body *is enjoying this*, she thought to herself and grunted, because that was the smartest comeback she could make.

"This was supposed to be punishment."

Despite the gag, she did her best to mumble, *Then why are you touching me like that when you know it's getting me off?*

He slid his fingers in and out a few times, gently, imitating coitus, and probed a little more.

Just as she was about to come, he said, "You're right. I don't really need to be doing this, if it's punishment," and pulled out.

Bastard. He *knew* how hard it was for her to come most of the time. She took whatever orgasms she could get, and she hated herself for it. She tried unsuccessfully to hump the washing machine.

"Don't worry," he said. "I won't use the paddle anymore."

That sounded ominous.

She nearly screamed when the fishing pole lashed into her, right on top of her raw backside. It was bamboo. She wasn't sure which was worse, bamboo, hickory, or birch - really, they were all awful, and she tried to avoid knowing the fine lines of difference between the woods. There was fun pain and not-so-fun pain, and she had decided long ago that everything made from wood was not fun.

He was precise in laying the thin parallel lines, working his way down from the top of her posterior down. The worst part was when the bamboo pole landed just above the backs of her knees. She had no padding there.

Her throat was raw. She hadn't screamed yet - she was too proud - but strangling her scream and converting it into a muffled *augh* made her sore.

She felt him shove something into her. His cock? No, not quite warm enough. It met no resistance. She was a river. Her body had betrayed her again; it always did. It didn't care how she felt. It was utterly single-minded. It didn't care how it got its orgasms, so long as they were good orgasms. Bizarrely, she felt her core start to throb in time with the thrusts. She realized that he was using her favorite dildo. It was fat and long. Most of her sex partners, regardless of gender, found it intimidating.

"Having fun yet?" he asked. "No, don't try to answer."

Once again, just as she was on the verge of coming, he stopped, sliding it out gently and slowly, taunting her.

"Don't worry. You'll get your chance, if you behave."

She couldn't kick him. Her ankles were not only manacled, but held with a cord to the nearby pipes.

"I want you to know what these next lashes are for. I'm going to hit you hard. I'll be surprised if you think it's fun... This one," he said, "is for ruining all of my shirts in the wash the one time you actually voluntarily did a load of laundry, shrinking them all and covering them with red stains from the lipstick you had in the pocket of your jeans."

It wasn't the bamboo cane anymore. It was something worse. She wasn't sure what it was. Whatever it was, it was hard and thin and extremely whippy. She moaned.

"This is for the pile of dirty dishes that's stacked up to the kitchen window... This is for the dust elephants... This one, and I'm going to make it a special one, is for all the crap you buy on eBay... This is for making me wear condoms..."

The list of complaints was not very long, but she was sure she was bleeding by the time he was done.

He paused to let her catch her breath; she was strangling on her tears, snot, and saliva. His arm was probably starting to get tired, anyway. Then he flipped her over.

"I'm not done yet," he said, pulling off her blindfold. The dim basement suddenly seemed blindingly bright to her. "I'm nowhere near done. I'm still pissed about having to wear condoms after years of trusting you to be on the pill." He unfastened the panic clasp at her ankle shackles. One of her legs remained tied to the laundry sink pipe. Yanking her legs open and holding her down by her right leg, the free one, he said, "This is for making me wear condoms. Don't think I'm going to just let that go. And no, don't close your eyes. You always close your eyes when we have sex. I want you to keep your eyes open and look at me, at what I'm doing to you. No, don't look away, because I'll only go harder on you. *Look at me.*"

His right hand fell down hard between her legs.

She jerked.

"No. You are not getting away from me. Don't try it. Don't even think about it," he murmured, as he proceeded to hammer at her. Smack. Smack.

He was holding her down too hard; trying to get away from the blows, which was automatic on her part, hurt her back. She kicked out at him and missed.

"That won't help you. I'll remember that. I think I'll remember it for at least twenty more smacks."

She moaned...

Eventually, his hand wasn't hitting her nether regions anymore. It couldn't, because it was inside them. How did it get there so quickly, so easily? She cursed her stupid, stupid body.

"I said look at me. Look at me, or I'll stop."

Since he had given her no choice, she watched him lower himself to the level of her groin, put his mouth close to her, gently exhale wet air on her, and establish contact between his mouth and tongue and her sex. She wanted to close her eyes when she felt the inevitable approach of the oncoming orgasm. She didn't think she could even come without closing her eyes - it wasn't physically possible for her. She didn't think... She felt herself spasm, hard, and cried out against it into the cloth gag that was still shoved in her mouth.

His hand rocked inside her gently, riding the waves of her orgasm until she was done, and pulled out slowly. His fingers lingered on the outside of her, touching her so delicately, so lightly, that losing herself in a happy, sated cloud was not an option, and making her groan with torment.

He ascended - *oh, rats* - and climbed onto the top of the ancient washing machine.

He tore off the gag.

"This," he said, "is for the countless times you've promised me a blowjob, and didn't deliver; or went down on me for a few brief seconds and stopped because you wanted 'real' sex."

He took her mouth.

She wasn't able to control him with her hands the way she liked to. She was used to boyfriends who were sensitive at the tip and who were perfectly fine with just a little sucking and teasing and hand work. Not he. He had always wanted to go all the way in. She had a gag reflex from hell, and tried to avoid triggering it; whoever had the notion that women enjoyed deep-throating men, anyway? She was hard-pressed to keep herself positioned in a way that kept him from going in all the way to the base of his cock, which she knew she couldn't handle.

He was stubborn, and methodical, and careful, and he started slow, but it didn't take long for him to start moving quickly and urgently.

And then he stopped, thank God.

Dismounted. Flipped her over again, so that she was once again prone. She felt some kind of hard wedge underneath her, brushing up against her clit, but also raising her hips. From behind her, she heard a wooden scraping sound as the nearby footstool got dragged into position.

"This," he said emphatically, "*is for making me have to use a bloody condom because you wanted to go off your birth control!*"

He plunged into her, making her groan again.

He was not wearing latex. She hoped fervently that he would either pull out at the last minute or go the anal route. Damn him. Then the washing machine began a spin cycle. Bloody hell. Who would have thought it? All the stereotypes about bored housewives who like to sit on the washing machine during its spin cycle were all true... Her breath escaped in gasps. She heard his breath get ragged. *No*, she thought, *no, what if I'm ovulating? I don't want to be pregnant...* He pulled out and entered her again, this time taking the tighter hole (*thank God*), which pushed her up against the wedge. The wedge vibrated merrily along with the manic washer. He slid in and out a few times and then, after one last and painfully hard thrust, he gasped and stopped, collapsing onto her.

A few moments later, after she had collected herself, she was able to say primly, "That wasn't punishment. Happy Valentine's Day."

Eventually, they burst out laughing. There was no other way they could have reacted, all things considered.

ANYTHING FOR A FRIEND

Here's the second story I am going to slap a content advisory onto.

It's a story that, like the television show Breaking Bad, *could never happen anywhere but in the United States. All other industrialized countries have state-supported medical care. Dying cancer patients in other countries do not need to worry about the economics of prolonging their lives with expensive treatments, nor do they need to worry about bankrupting their survivors with medical bills, hospice bills, etc.*

As I type this, a new presidential administration is on its way. Our incoming president has sworn to end the Affordable Care Act and marketplace plans. While ACA plans are not as affordable as they were when they were first introduced, they are still something for people who can't get affordable coverage in other ways. Subsidies are available for those people who can't afford premiums and the worst of the cost-sharing.

And now it's about to be drowned in the bathtub, as the saying goes.

There may be other casualties of this administration. The Department of Education is to be dissolved, its funds redistributed in block grants to the states to decide how they want to spend it. Pell Grants for low-income students who cannot afford college tuition will probably be abolished, too. Why have grants to pay for legitimate higher education when a free online university that teaches dumbed-down right-wing indoctrination will soon be available to all American citizens? And then there are student loans, which are to be "restructured." A part of that is that student loan forgiveness programs are going to be abolished. So are income-adjusted repayment plans, including the REPAYE plan I'm on. If I can't be grandfathered in, my student loan repayments will be jacked up to slightly more than $3,000 per month, which will render me destitute, and my family homeless. So, how much is left on the mortgage? How much is the face value of my life insurance policy? No, no, let's not go there. It's practical, but it's supposed to be unthinkable.

Financial problems should not be terminal. That is obscene on so many levels. Things are "unthinkable" for a reason...

This is a thought experiment about brutal, unjust, unnecessary, existential economic terror, and what can come of it.

It does not end happily.

For the record, I do not advocate suicide as a solution to these sorts of problems – assisted, like the suicide portrayed in the story, or otherwise.

A breeze brushes past me: soft breath on my skin. It's nearly dark. The fireflies are out; so are the crickets, which make their ritual evening serenade as I test the ground beneath me for softness. This is not a good place to set up the tent. It's too rocky. The rocks might come in handy later for something, but I don't want to set up a tent on them, cot or no cot. A bit further up is a pine grove, where the ground is soft and springy and smells vaguely of incense. It's secluded, and dense at the edges with undergrowth. Perfect. A perfect place for a June night spent under the sky, in the middle of Upper Peninsula nowhere, near the banks of Lake Superior.

Actually, I've always hated camping. It's not that I dislike the great outdoors per se, but the pollen and so on give me allergic fits, and that combined with insects tasting me for sweetness gives me a feeling that my skin is crawling, and I loathe the hard work that is involved in setting up a camp and staying there for only a night or two, only to strike it. Let's just say I've always been an indoor person and leave it at that. This night is no exception; on an aesthetic level I enjoy the crickets and fireflies and mellow dusk, but the rest of me curses at having to set up a tent in the dark.

"Have you set up camp in the dark before?"

"You haven't?"

"No. I'm sorry. I get my boyfriends and girlfriends to do that kind of thing for me."

He snorts.

"It figures."

"I know. I'm pretty much useless except for one or two things. It must pain you, but can you live with it?"

We look at each other.

"Ollie, Ollie, in come free!"

I creep out from under the tarp that covers the wood pile in the next-door neighbor's back yard, and saunter over to the porch that Mike and I have established as "base." This time, I'd managed to pick a perfect hiding place. About time. He usually finds me, and he's a faster runner than I am, so when he's It, if he finds me, I'm as good as caught.

"Where the heck were you?"

"Over there. Under the tarp."

He looks. There's a lump in the tarp showing the shape of my body. I'm amazed he never found me – that hiding place wasn't nearly as good as I thought it was, now that I can see it from here.

"Wow, cool! It looks like someone's hid a dead body under there!"

My mother opens the kitchen door and calls out, "Come in, you two. It's getting dark."

"Jesus, Mike, you don't seriously want to go through with this, do you?"

"We've gone over this before. My doctor said the cancer's too far gone to treat - he doesn't blame me for waiting since I don't have insurance, but at best, he can slow things down a few more months, assuming I can somehow come up with the money to pay for treatments. There are charities that might help, maybe. The other two doctors that I asked for second and third opinions said pretty much the same thing. One of them wanted to talk to me about hospice care as an alternative to chemo and radiation. *Hospice care.* Shit, I don't want to stick around for that. My brother will get stuck with the bills later. That's like ten thousand a month for every month I manage to not die of cancer. And again, there are charities that might help, maybe, if I make enough requests... No. Send me out. Send me out big. Help me out with a scream." He grimaces a little, and mutters, "You did pack all the stakes and shit, didn't you?"

Yes. This time, for once, I packed efficiently and thoroughly, remembering the essentials but leaving the frou-frou out, checking and re-checking the supplies because I had to be careful to use no recoverable list of any kind. Everything is there, even the lantern and the tiki torches and fuel so that we will not have to battle the darkness. I'm trying hard not to let him see how nervous I am. I'm too scared. I want to make this absolutely perfect for him. I'm only going to get this one chance; it has to be right. What if I'm not good enough? What if he hates what I've planned? It's terrible, the stage fright. I always get it on a first date, but it's never been this bad.

And I'm hungry. Oh God. I've never been this hungry. I've gone without for over a year, and even then, it wasn't like this. I suppose I shouldn't find it surprising that my hunger is up, but I can be ashamed of it.

Surely he can tell.

Surely he can also tell that I don't want to be here.

I don't suppose that really matters.

He pulls out the tarp, then the tent and the stakes and the mallet, the lantern and the torches, and starts setting up camp.

Meanwhile, I busy myself with things like rope, the latex bodysuit and cap we chose to cover any hair and skin cells I might shed, the gloves, the needles and blades, the candles and matches, the gym bag with its assortment of goodies (I pull out a rubber squeaky rat and a short steel-tipped flogger, in addition to a riding crop that I bought online just a week ago) and similar necessities.

I go over the general course of the evening's activities to myself as he pounds stakes. I like having an outline, even though I usually end up deviating from it a little.

I finish preparing the scene at about the same time that he finishes setting up the tent, fire buckets, and lanterns.

"Do you want a fire?" I ask. "It's going to get cold in a bit. Fires draw attention, but they do warm things up."

"Do you see any other campers?"

I smile grimly to myself. "True enough. Let's get a fire going over by the rocks."

Mrs. Winthrop stood patiently and silently at the front of the classroom, which was her way of getting our attention. Oddly enough, it always worked.

There was a boy standing next to her.

"This is Mike Morris," she said. "His family just moved here, and he's been assigned to our class. He doesn't know anybody yet. Would somebody like to be his friend and show him around?"

A few arms went up, but I made myself hard to ignore.

"Me! ME!" I cried, waving my arm around.

I didn't have many friends of my own, either, in the second grade, and I didn't have the excuse of being new.

That was the start of us. It wasn't long before teachers and other grownups started calling us "The Dynamic Duo" and "The Wonder Twins." Our classmates had some less flattering names to call us, but we ignored them, and eventually, our classmates ignored us.

We lost touch when we went to college on different coasts, but thanks to Facebook, we found each other again. We couldn't believe our luck. We'd finally found each other, after so many years. And as it turned out, we had a lot in common.

We swore we'd never leave each other again.

Despite the relative warmth of the earlier part of the evening, a chill soon follows the darkness. We sit by the fire warming our hands. I pull out a bottle of rare, extremely aged Talisker – a good portion of my monthly wages – and pour some of the precious liquid into a plastic Thermos cap. "Here. Happy birthday. Drink up." None for me, of course; I need coordination. I am one of those people who believes that driving drunk is never acceptable, be the driven thing a vehicle or another person.

After he drinks his whiskey, grunting with what I hope is awed appreciation but what in actuality is probably just alcohol up the windpipe, I pick up the rope and a small bag of equipment. "Ready when you are."

He's ready.

We make our way to another part of the pine grove, a section without the creeping scrub trees that seem to have invaded the other parts of the grove.

I wrap the trunk with duct tape – he said that he liked discomfort, but I don't think pine sap and a crackful of bark count as "good" discomfort – and note with satisfaction that the trees are spaced absolutely perfectly. That should help. I'm going to start with his back, so I get him to face the trunk before I start tying his ankles together.

"I can hold still."

"I'm sure you can," I reply with a purr.

"You didn't tell me you planned to tie me up."

"That's right, I didn't. I know you think you won't try to run away from me, but I don't want to take any chances, hmm? The last thing I want to do is take up half the night staging a scene from The Blair Witch Project. By the way, I don't have a rifle, so we'd better pray that we won't get attacked by any bears, which would be just my luck…"

I finish tying his ankles and work on stretching out his arms, fastening them to the nearest trees. He's almost suspended. Not quite. Almost. I studied my old Girl Scout knot guide for months and practiced, fumbling over and over until I could finally get the knots right, all in preparation for this. It's not quite crucifixion, what I'm doing to him, but it's pretty damn close. His arms I draw to either side, and slightly back over shoulder level, which is incredibly strenuous, because it pulls on the muscles. It looks lovely, of course, but it's not the sort of position you want to keep somebody in for very long unless you plan to cause serious muscle and tendon damage. It's definitely not a position for a heavy or pear-shaped person to be put into, so it's just as well he is not shaped like an apple or a pear. If it gets really bad, I can tighten the rope underneath his hips to give him some extra support, but for now, I leave it slack so that he dangles.

He's already starting to struggle for air. I hadn't realized that the effect would be so quick.

I pull out the steel-tipped cat: no warm-up for this boy. He likes pain.

He'll get it.

"Yell all you want," I say quietly, "because there's no one near to hear you scream."

Ready, aim, fire.

The tips land on his flesh, on his gaunt frame. Already I'm drawing blood. Too late I realize that he'll probably get chewed up by mosquitoes, and I hope that it will enhance the whole Gestalt experience because I'm not about to stop now. He hasn't started screaming yet, although he's grunting a lot, and the blood is running a lot because of the whiskey thinning it. Oh, yes, that was deliberate. I do think of these things in advance, you know.

I'm getting into a good rhythm now. The scary thing is that I don't have to hit very hard. I'm afraid of what might happen if I use this thing with full force.

I don't want to turn his back to meat – not yet – so I lay off the flogger for a while and pick up the rat.

The rat makes an absurd little squeak in my hand.

"Meet Ratbert," I say in a murmur, and I make the rat squeak again shortly before I use the round, ringed tail to bite into his arse. Ratbert is at least as nasty as the steel-tipped cat if used right.

My nastiest toy of all is actually a segmented plastic jump rope. It's amazing what you can pick up at a dollar bargain store. I hope I get a chance to use the jump rope later; I wouldn't dream of using it on anybody but a serious pain junkie, and I haven't met any other real pain junkies, at least nobody that I want to play with.

He's breathing raggedly, in hoarse coughing gasps. No. I don't want him to asphyxiate to death. I stop – the welts on his arse aren't quite bleeding freely the way his back is – and undo the rope on one of his wrists, pulling on the rope until I reach him so that he doesn't fall. Repeat on the other side. He hasn't collapsed yet. He's just having trouble breathing. His back is very wet; my latex gloves come away covered in blood. I don't lick the blood off; it's not fresh anymore after it's left the body. It's also cold. I prefer to drink blood when it's warm.

This shaking, pale puppet needs to be kissed. I put my lips carefully to his wounds. Must kiss them to make it better. Must kiss them. Must – ah, how sweet, and fiery on my tongue – I can taste his craving, it's like pungent fruit. I can also taste his fear. Yeah, okay, so I'm a sick puppy. So is he. That's what we like about each other, isn't it? Anyway, you'd be surprised how many vampires there are in the world. It's not just the blood, it's what's in the blood, the energy and passion; but the blood itself is divine.

I'm not done with him yet. He's not done with me. We have a long way to go.

I turn him around so that he's facing me, then stretch him again; more tightly. Now he's upright and leaned back against the trunk instead of stretched forward. It's quite beautiful to behold: a short, wiry, scrawny, and utterly masculine man, a good five inches shorter than I am at least, on tiptoe, stretched out as tight as can be, fighting for breath – and as hard as a rock.

I like this.

I reach out for him and, pulling hard on his member, feeling it stiffen even more at my touch, lean close to him, and whisper in his ear. "Are we having fun yet?"

"You know I don't get off on this. I'm not aroused."

"Me neither," I say, stroking back and forth lovingly. "Not in the slightest. Perish the thought." I squeeze. His cock twitches. "Are you sure you're not getting off, just a teensy bit?"

"This wasn't what I'd had in mind..."

I lean close to his ear.

"I know. You don't like to be dominated. You don't usually like sex to be a part of the activity when you scene, either. This wasn't something I'd originally planned for you. And yet I want you now. I need you... I'm having a very hard time holding back, you know. I have you where I want you, and I do *not* want to let go." I trace his shaft with my fingernail and caress the head of his cock with my other hand. "And whether you want it or not, you're straining under my hands. How *delicious*."

My voice quavers. I'm riding high on nerves. This is not good.

"Keep going?" I ask.

"Yes."

I smile. "But rape isn't nice, now is it? I'd better stop... This is really hard for me. Excuse the pun."

I pull away and pick up my new crop. It's time to give the crop a good christening.

He's starting to look really pale. His breath comes out in rattling gasps now. The blood has run down his back and chest, and dried, and congealed; his cock is red, and raw in some spots where I hit him over and over several times in a row, hard. He came twice. Not bad for someone who says he doesn't have a sex drive, and who doesn't find me at all attractive. The crop indeed got a good christening before I pulled out the whip again.

His flesh looked like ribbons by the time I had to stop to rest. Something in me came out, finally, and howled and demanded to be fed, something that I keep chained and controlled, and it got loose and I don't even know how long I whipped him, just that it felt much too good and I don't even know if I would have stopped if he'd begged for mercy, which, thank goodness, he hadn't.

I try to avoid letting myself lose control like that. I don't believe in letting go. This is supposed to be "safe, sane, and consensual;" what we do tonight is neither safe nor sane. As for consensual...

What if he were to cry safeword? Would I even listen, at this point? I'd like to think so, but if he'd begged for mercy a few minutes ago I might not even have heard him. I did give him a safeword, of course, only an idiot wouldn't, but what's the point of having a safeword if I can't hear it?

Do I get a safeword?

No, of course not. Cancer doesn't use safewords. And Mike is the most stubborn person I've ever known.

Slowly, I ease him down from the rig. He can't stand up by himself. He's on the verge of passing out, so I support him. It's not that hard. He weighs less than I do. I can count his ribs by running my fingers over them. The welts, too. A book of Braille.

Clinging to each other, conspirators to a crime, we stagger over to the rocks.

He doesn't have enough strength to complain when I break out the manacles and set about restraining him again. I stretch him out to his full length, lengthwise this time, and pin the wrist and ankle cuffs down with pegs. These I secure with little lines and stakes. I need a good canvas, so I don't secure his entire body, but I do lash down his arms and the lower parts of his legs, and his neck. I think of Gulliver in Lilliput, only Gulliver had his clothes on, and my partner is naked. It's close enough to the fire that we're still warm. I don't want him to shiver. Shivering would get in the way of what I want to do just as much as squirming would.

Should I blindfold him?

No. I want him to see exactly what I'm about to do.

I've never actually done this before, either. I don't suppose it will make a difference, really, all things considered, but I'm still sweating bullets. I'm so afraid of screwing up. I'm also afraid of my tools: in addition to my usual razor blades, an artist's knife, and a few other things that fit into a plastic zip pouch, I have packages of needles. Acupuncture needles. Piercing needles. I usually avoid them because I have this hang-up about never doing to other people what I wouldn't be willing to endure myself, and so the thought of using them makes me very nervous. The only parts of my body I've had pierced are my ears, which I got done at a play party, plus another two holes with color-coded studs in my left earlobe that I had a professional install. I have no desire for anything more painful and intimate than that.

However, he said that the only thing he wanted out of this evening for himself, aside from the scripted ending, was extreme pain. I'm not really an imaginative person, so I'd make a lousy torturer; I couldn't think of very many things to do to him that wouldn't break bones, remove body parts, or otherwise maim him. There are some things that I don't think I could do unless I were fighting for my life. Besides, I suspect that he wouldn't get any emotional satisfaction out of ripped tendons or broken bones or anything like that, painful though these things might be. There's a difference between good pain and bad pain.

The clamps go on first. Japanese clover clamps – the kind that get tighter when you pull on them. I've tested them on myself, and I can't handle them for longer than ten seconds. I put them on the usual places: nipples, balls.

I'm ready. I show him the needles.

He starts shivering. I hope it's not shock.

I might be hoping for too much.

"Don't shiver," I say. "It gets in the way and makes things hurt more. Wait a minute. That's what you want, isn't it?"

I start with the piercing needles – I hung out in a tattoo parlor and quietly apprenticed myself to one of the piercing artists there two months earlier, just to learn how to do this right – and look for loose flesh, because for the most part, whatever is loose can be pierced temporarily. Most of the flesh and cartilage of his ears is pierced already.

So I slowly push the needles through the less obvious spots: the skin of the upper chest, the upper arms, the lower arms, the upper thighs.

He wears armor now, armor that has been woven into his very skin. I'm glad of the restraints that hold him down. because his body is shuddering in hard, terrible waves.

I smile sweetly, although he isn't looking at my face and can't see me smile.

"Do you know what the Aztec warriors used to do?"

"What?" he asks through clenched teeth.

"They pierced themselves exactly the way I'm about to do to you now, to make personal offerings to their war god. Most Aztec sacrifices were personal. They didn't involve other people."

"How nice. You know how I feel about religion."

"Yes. I know. The same way you feel about sex. I thought you'd want to do this for the sheer fun of it anyway."

I only have five piercing needles left, out of two hundred. I've been reserving them for this.

I take the first of these five needles and insert it into the top flesh of his abused and now mostly flaccid penis. And for the first time tonight, for the first time after being flayed and strangled by crucifixion to within an inch of his life, then beaten, then turned into a writhing pin cushion, he screams, a high girlish scream of agony.

I wait until he is done screaming, then I push in the second needle, a little closer to the head of the penis.

He screams for each needle.

By the time I am done, he is hoarse and wet, and the shaft of his cock is bloody.

I am having far too much fun. I was not supposed to enjoy it this way. Something about this night has released my monster, and it is out romping, howling, screaming for orgasm. I will never do this again, I remind myself. Never. Never will he. Aren't we having fun?

He is limp, and white, the color of skimmed milk. He isn't trembling as hard, but his body is shivering; if a sine wave had a human form, it might look something like this. I think he might be about at the end of his rope. Actually, if the circumstances were different, I'd be calling an ambulance about now.

"Be glad you aren't an Aztec," I mutter, "they used huge cactus spines for genital piercing, rather than these thin little needles."

He curses. It sounds like a whimper. Good. There's still plenty of him there.

"Dear," I whisper, "I'm not done yet."

My canvas opens his eyes again, disbelieving. My God. He actually looks a little worried. There's a manic fire in his eyes that I realize for fear. I start to reach for his head, to stroke his hair and reassure him. But something in me stops. I don't want him to be afraid, any more than I want him to be here at all – but I need it. I need it so bad.

"Stay with me," I whisper, "don't fade out on me yet. I'm not letting you go. Not now."

I pull out the Exacto knife, with its fresh blade that I had loaded earlier while wearing my latex gloves, and begin to trace designs around the piercings. I did this with woad at a historical reenactor's camp a couple of years ago, painting swirls, knots, lines and waves. Now I engrave the same – triskeles and waves and dots, old ritual markings, tattoos of an earlier, bloodier age. Often the blade slashes against raw flesh. He isn't screaming, but despite himself, he's crying. After a while, he stops trying to hold it back and gives over to it.

Then he writhes. This probably hurts him just as bad, because his mangled back is pressed up against sharp rocks. He doesn't writhe often, but sometimes he can't help it. It's terrible to watch, and beautiful.

I'm not distracted by the possibility of orgasm anymore. I'm probably on the edge, but I'm busy doing other things now and I can't be bothered with my bodily reactions. I know only the blood and the design, the writhing and moans of pain, the firelight and the smell of pine. The awful aloneness of the night, the night that at least for now, we own.

I stop and look at my handiwork. Somewhere, underneath the needles and the cuts and the welts, is a human being, but you'd have to look awfully hard.

"I wish you could see yourself."

He looks at me again. He's not glaring at me. He's not crying anymore, either. I'm not sure I even recognize what's in his eyes. Whatever it is, it's capable of a smile, so I know there's a stubborn part of him that hasn't quite succumbed yet. Amazing. Well, he did describe himself as an unbreakable toy. And they say vampires are the ones who have all the constitution points. Not this time. I would have passed out long ago.

"You should see *yourself*," he says with a laugh, and I realize what that look is.

He laughs, hysterical and triumphant, and I don't laugh with him because I'm focusing on what comes next. One of us has to drive. As I said, I don't drive drunk. I have nothing against other people getting drunk while I'm driving, though.

The needles all have to come out. He knows this.

After another fifteen minutes or so of undoing my pincushion, it's time to take off the clamps. They've been on for way too long. "You know how long you've been wearing these?" I ask as I prepare to pinch them open. I don't care how much he likes pain, I'm not going to yank them off.

He'll get plenty of pain anyway. They've been on for almost forty-five minutes. Long enough to make him scream again when the clamps are removed and the blood comes rushing back.

I let him get his breath for about a minute, then pick up his last ordeal for the evening – a beeswax candle about three inches in diameter. I usually avoid beeswax because it's dangerously hot. It's been burning for the duration of the piercing and cutting. I wonder what bad second-degree burns feel like on abused skin. Awful, I suspect. Under other circumstances, I'd say that the point of this might ostensibly be to cauterize the bleeding from the worse cuts, but we both know there's no point to that, so it's just about gratuitous pain.

But ah, no, none of the pain tonight is gratuitous. It's there for its own sake.

This will be my last chance, so give me your worst like I've always wanted, he said, and I asked, are you sure you want that? My worst is pretty bad. Do you really know what you're asking for?

My dear partner in crime. This will hurt me more than it hurts you – but not just yet.

I stand and raise my arm, and the candle, high. The drippings won't fall as precisely as they otherwise could, but there should be a *little* less damage this way.

It's over. It's over. I get him loose. He trembles in my arms, despite the heat of the fire. Now I know he is in shock, well into it, not just on the edge, because he seems to be almost nodding off. But he's still fighting it – he keeps snapping back and blinking hard.

"Do you still want to go into the tent?" I ask.

I stare at him in a concerned sort of way while he bores holes into me with his eyes.

He nods.

"Give me another drink," he says, and I give him a whole cupful of Scotch. What the hell. It can't hurt now. Down the hatch, it goes.

I watch his throat work.

Then, after a few minutes of looking into the fire, watching the phantoms appear in the smoke, making me wonder if he's succumbed and lost consciousness, which would let me off the hook – for a while anyway – he says, "All right. Now I'm ready."

He needs to be held up, so I hold him while he stumbles into the cheap little dome tent.

It's dark inside. I turn on the flashlight. It's not light enough. The light of the campfire flickers outside, and that, too, is not enough.

He lies on the cot.

"Are you *sure* you want me to do this?" I ask. There is a point where there will be no turning back. Yes, I know, it's an old, old cliché, but for once the cliché is based on something real.

"Still yes."

"I don't want to do it. *I don't even want to be here -*"

"Stop making this about you, for once. It's not about you."

He glares at me. Daring me, begging me, I don't know anymore. Probably both.

I sigh. "All right, then."

I pull out the straight razor that I found in the antique shop six months ago and place it to his throat.

My hands start to shake. My God. I'm actually doing it. After everything, I still hadn't expected him to want to go through with it. As a friend I hate myself for what I am about to do, hate him for making me give him up, although I can tell myself that this isn't really suicide, it's just checking out early, as it were - he's already been told he's dying. As myself, simply myself – I must confess to a certain curiosity after all the angst and drama is said and done. There. I guess I am a monster after all. Who but a monster would help a friend kill himself? And actually look forward to it, even if only in part, a smallish part at that?

"I'm ready when you are," I say.

He nods, a single short nod, and I slice. Carotid. Jugular.

The blood is everywhere, which is one reason I put on the latex suit before our evening started.

I bend down to drink. Warmth takes me over. It feels like sacrilege, and sacrament, all at once. I've never had a life. I've drunk blood and sapped energy, of course, but I've never actually taken a life. Oh God. The sweet metallic taste devours me, fills my mouth, I can't have it all or I'll make myself sick, I have to be careful; I bury my face in it and absorb the awful sensation of him, his clammy skin and hot stubborn spark, the life leaving his body, his last gasps of breath deserting him, the rushing and the drowning and then the cold oblivion of him being gone, simply gone.

The blood no longer tastes sweet.

I want to cry. I will never see him again, never write him again. Never play with him again.

Few people understand me and accept me for who and what I really am. They sugar coat me, or I give myself to them with a spoonful of sugar because I know they can't handle the real me. Or I make myself ugly, to drive them away, or I make fun of this thing inside myself because humor defangs anything.

Mike never thought I was horrible. He liked me. When we were kids, it was us against the world and all its bullies, and there were so many of them; as adults we found we had something together that few people share, an extremity that seemed to be uniquely ours – and now he's gone, all because of me. I don't believe in dying alone, the loneliness and coldness of it – when I die I want to die in the arms of someone who loves me, if I have the chance. I wanted to give him that kindness, at least. I also don't believe in letting opportunities go to waste, and what an incredible opportunity comes from the death of a desperate masochist who begs you to take his life, saying he'll just do it himself anyway if he doesn't have help. He would have followed through on that, too. He doesn't believe in making dramatic but empty threats.

Didn't believe, now.

Finally, a chance to be completely myself, no holds barred.

And it killed him. Just like he wanted.

I can't cry. I want to, but I can't. My eyes are dry, and my throat is numb.

I'm still buzzing from the blood and the incredible energy of his life that he breathed into me. He is in my veins. He is with me forever. It's not the same, though. Even his after-trace cannot fill the absolute loneliness that is left in his wake.

PARLIAMENT OF ROOKS

This "just-so story" written in the medieval European style of a "dream vision" is a pastiche. Thanks for some elements of the story must be given not just to Geoffrey Chaucer, and to Dante Alighieri, but also to Virgil and to Neil Gaiman.

I have a confession to make: I am a hopeless melancholic. I do not mean this in the sense that I am always depressed and pessimistic, although this is indeed frequently true. No, when I say I am melancholic, I mean this in the classical sense of the word. I wear dark colors that make my skin look pale and jaundiced. I philosophize. I am prone to strange maladies that no one knows quite what to make of - when I contract the flu, or some other conventional illness, then I am hit harder than most people, and I lie in bed speculating on death and life-in-death. I am a bit too morbid for my own good.

I'm introverted, although I've learned to hide my preference for being alone behind a mask. I'm terrible at cocktail parties, though, because my usual party behavior is to find the library and get lost in it unless I have close friends that I know and am actually happy to greet. (My close friends are apt to join me in the library, being much like me in many ways).

Perhaps that's the most annoying thing about me - I am a scholar at heart, and I cannot really imagine having to live outside an ivory tower. I hate the real world. I'd much rather devote my attention to words. To most people, preferring fantasy and speculation to reality is an unforgivable sin. It smacks of immaturity to them, if not actual antisocial proclivities. I won't deny either of these qualities in me - I'm probably immature, and certainly, I'm quite antisocial once you get to know me, and my fantasy life is so vivid that it has a life all its own.

It should come as no surprise, then, that a few nights ago while poring over Chaucer's *Parliament of Foules*, I fell asleep and had a most interesting dream. So real it was, that I could scarcely tell whether I was awake or in a sleeping state.

This is highly unusual for me - since I am so accustomed to the various varieties of dream consciousness: daydreaming, sleeping, vision quest, and so on, I usually have a shaman-like ability to detect when I am dreaming, and to navigate and even control the dream a little. I think I should mention here that I almost never read books one at a time. I usually have five or six of them near my bed. No doubt this, too, had an effect on my dream.

It was not Scipio who came to me in my dream, though, but Geoffrey Chaucer himself.

"You have for some time been pondering in your mind the nature of love," he said to me, his eye twinkling the faintest bit. "You have been asking for a guide, and behold! I am here."

I took a look about me once again. There seemed to be a gate made of horn, and it was blank above.

"Are there not two gates?" I asked my guide. I've read Dante.

"There are. We have passed through the gate of courtly love already. Why else do you think I am here by your side?"

That quite figures, I thought silently.

It was amazing that I did not see the forest until that moment. In dreams, I suppose, all things are hidden until our eyes first begin to look for them. A primeval glade of tall conifers occupied the land as far as the eye could see; the trunks of two trees were as wide as houses, and soared up into the air so far that it was indeed difficult to tell when tree ended and sky began. A sharp perfume was invading my nostrils. I smelled pine, and sap, and wood, and moss. This is the scent of youth and abundant health that aerosol cleansers try, and fail, to capture. There is no way to capture a scent so rich - perfumes cannot be as fresh as the scents they imitate. You might as well try to bottle the essence of a unicorn, which (I have been told) is a peculiarly nonmammalian scent of mint, lavender, and rosemary.

A raven flew by, calling out in a croaking voice. It was white. It wore a blue ribbon wrapped about its right leg. Long after it had flown past, I saw before me the trailing ribbon and heard the hoarse, raucous cry.

The trees echoed. Strangely, there was no sound in the forest but the terrible echo of the raven's cry. No other birds invaded the silence; no breeze made the trees moan. My breathing suddenly seemed very loud. It was rude to my ears; it seemed too human, too ragged for this world.

I turned to my guide for help.

"Come," he said, "or we will miss the parliament."

"Is there to be a parliament of birds?"

"Yes. Rooks."

I had never attended a parliament of rooks, or a parliament of any other fowl, for that matter, although I had encountered such parliaments in my reading. I wondered if we would even be allowed to attend.

Rooks are a peculiar species of bird. Their very nature betrays their general untrustworthiness; to "rook" means to cheat or steal, and a "rookery" (that is, a place where hundreds of rooks make their dwelling) is an old word for a ghetto of thieves and prostitutes.

Rooks are among the most social of birds. They like to flock together. They have a highly developed language, compared to other birds, and like parrots can be trained to mimic human speech. Most peculiarly of all, their collective name - a "parliament of rooks" - comes from a custom they have of gathering in a field. Thousands of rooks will converge for no apparent reason. A space in the middle of the birds will be formed, and a single rook will be found standing in that space.

The rook will caw, and caw some more. This can go on for hours.

At the end of some specified time limit, there will be a brief silence, and then the rooks will do one of two things. Either they will all fly away never to converge on that particular field again, or they will set themselves on the lone rook and peck it to death. It appears to be a sort of trial, hence the name.

(Members of the *Corvidae* family all have unusual names for their groupings. They don't form flocks. A group of crows is called a "murder" of crows. Magpies come in "tidings," and ravens in "unkindnesses." This family of birds is traditionally associated with madness, death, and the supernatural).

I expressed my fear that our presence would frighten the rooks away.

"Don't worry," Chaucer reassured me, "they won't detect us. If any of them see us, they will think us to be rooks like them."

We had been walking through the forest for some time, and now we came to a field of high grass. Suddenly, the air was full of noise - cawing, jabbering; it was difficult to tell whether I was hearing a large group of raucous birds, or a large crowd of excited people. I could not understand a word that was spoken, and the noise was so great that I winced and had to cover my ears. Eventually, though, the horrid sounds ceased, and I could see the lone rook standing before me.

The rook began.

"You have observed that we are all compelled to mate, to produce offspring. This is the commandment of Eros, who is the god of desire, who wishes all living beings to perpetuate their own species. However, there is a certain creature that walks on two legs and yet has no wings; it is craftier than even our race, having the ability to make tools, even to steal fire from the very heavens. This you know. Most of us have encountered these creatures at some point in our existence - we have all, at one time in our lives, flown past their shining and terrible cities, which are friendly to no creature. However, what is less known to we of the flying kingdoms is the fact that these creatures often feel an emotion called *being in love* when they desire; this is the thing that separates them from us. This is their curse. It is by the command of Eros himself, he who commands all living beings to desire a partner with whom to couple.

"Once, there were no two-legged creatures in the world. There were only the various kingdoms - the winged kingdom, the water kingdom, the kingdom of furry land-crawlers, and the kingdom of scaly land-crawlers. Eros was bored one day, and so he decided to create a new kingdom. However, he thought it would be more prudent to create his kingdom in small numbers at first, and so he made three creatures from clay and water and a drop of his own blood. Two of these new creatures were male, and one was female.

"He observed their interaction. They seemed to be quite social, capable of more speech than any of his other creations so far, and quite willing to band together for warmth and comfort and protection. They shared their food, their shelter, and each other. At first this gave Eros much amusement, but then he realized that their willingness to share was brought on by necessity rather than by frivolous desires; he had made his new creatures too weak, for they possessed no claws, no fangs, no camouflaging colors or scaly armor. He had not yet been able to make a creation that experienced desire without need. This plagued him, for he wanted more than anything to create a creature of pure will and desire - a creature made in his image. It had been for this purpose that he had added his own blood to his creation.

"Desiring to free them of the shackles of necessity, he gave them a new gift: the gift of reason. They could now think clearly and quickly, and make decisions in a split second, even without instinct such as ours. Or they could sit and ponder, taking time to come to a decision. It would be their *choice*. They could also invent tools, now, to keep their enemies at bay. No longer would they be forced to huddle in fright; they could emerge from their hiding places for longer periods of time, and not just to forage better but also to explore.

"The female - whose name some say was Lily - was the craftiest of all. Perhaps Eros made her craftier, gave her more of the gift, because he admired her beauty. She was a most fine creation. At any rate, she said to herself, 'We need a weapon that will make us not mere animals, but gods.' For such as we are called in their tongue: *animals*. The blood of these creatures is godlike and proud and always demands to reunite with its creator, detaching itself from its own natural place in the world. 'We have sharpened sticks to hunt with, rocks to hammer or cut with; but we need more, if we are ever to create, to be as our father. How did he create us?'

"One of the males - I am told his name was Aron - answered, 'Out of clay, and water, and his own blood; he shaped us, baked us in a kiln, and then set us out in the sun.'

'Exactly,' said Lily. 'The kiln, the sun - they are hot. We must have fire. We need fire to create. To forge. Is it not fire that we feel in our loins, when we need to couple?'

'But how are we to get fire?' asked the other male, whose name was Cadwel.

'We must steal lightning from the heavens.'

"And so Lily dressed herself up in garlands of flowers until her beauty was such that it made her lovers ache to see her, indeed caused them to cast seed on the spot; and so, dressed in flowers, she went on a quest for the dwelling of Eros.

"Long was her quest, and perilous. She faced terrible heat and freezing cold; her stomach cried for hunger when she could not find food; great cats hunted her and forced her to fight them for her life. She searched through jungles, and plains, and deserts.

"Finally, her search bore her to a high mountain, and the top of the mountain was wreathed in clouds. Hard was the climb, but she knew that beyond the clouds was the object of her search; and so she climbed with determination, forcing herself to go on even when her feet were ripped to shreds by sharp stones. But at long last, she stood before a cottage made of marble and rubies. This was the home of Eros, and she knocked at his door.

'I am a gift from the five kingdoms,' she called out. 'Come and accept me, or send me back if I am displeasing.'

"Eros answered the summons. He beheld her and desired her, and he took her into his arms to have his way with her. Such was his delight that he was driven to couple with her again and again, even into the small hours of the night; such was her skill in disguise that he did not even recognize his own creation, but took her to be some new creature - a nymph of the forest, perhaps. He was so filled and so charmed, in fact, that he was convinced that here at last was his perfect mate. Lily accepted his ardor, even fed it until he fainted from the intensity of his own passion. While he was unconscious, she left him in his bed, and searched his dwelling until at last she found his forge, at which point she took a bolt of lightning and forced it into a rock, which became a glowing ember; with Eros' golden tongs, she placed the ember in a sack lined with fleece and magic spells, so the ember would burn without dying, but would nevertheless not burn through the sack. I do not know how she did this, for this is a mystery that we creatures of the earth are denied. But she grabbed the sack and fled into the night, making her long journey back home while Eros slept in his unnatural trance.

"At last, she arrived home, and explained to her lovers (who had been frantic for her) how to tend the fire that she had stolen. Soon they had a merry hearth-fire, and were able to cook meat over it and stay warm.

"Lily began to experiment with various substances: clay, and wood, and grass, and so on, and she made marvelous things: urns of clay in which to carry water, pipes and flutes and drums that made strange noises, lamps of animal fat and clay and grass rope that could be lit at night to provide light in the darkness. At last, her labors began to attract the attention of a magpie.

"Magpies are natural spies, being both very curious and very garrulous. The magpie flew instantly to Eros to tell his secret.

'My lord,' said the magpie, 'there is a creature on two legs tending a fire, and she makes strange tools and smoked meat over it.'

"When Eros heard this, he became very angry indeed. He had been desiring his nymph for some time, you see; he had been filled with so much passion and longing that it had made him weak and delirious. Now he realized that he had been tricked by one of his very own creations - played for a *fool!* - and he desired to inflict some of his own pain on her.

"He came to the dwelling place of his created children, blazing his anger so that he resembled a small, brilliant sun. Cadwel and Aron, who were ashamed, instantly hid in the small cave that was their home; but Lily stood by the fire, unafraid and unashamed. It was her nature to be bold; that was how she had been made. As perhaps I said before, of the three two-legged creatures, she most resembled her creator, having been gifted with the greatest portion of his blood.

'Where did you get this fire?' he demanded. 'I did not give you this fire.'

"It is the nature of any creature gifted with cunning to try and bluff its way out of a predicament. 'I trapped some lightning after a storm,' she said.

"This annoyed Eros even further. 'You lie! You came to me and stole the fire from me, disguised as a love-gift!'

'As a what?'

"Here Eros saw the means to punish his children.

'You say you do not know what a love-gift is? Oh, pitiful creature! Sad and beautiful thing! You are so like me - you who walk on two legs and think rather than acting on instinct! *I would have given the fire to you, had you only asked! For I love you!* If you only knew how I loved you then! I loved you before I even desired you. When you came to me from the heat... And then you left me senseless, and I did not realize that it was you I sickened for until a magpie came and told me of your forge, at which point I realized all. You are so like me. And yet, unaware of your nature, you feel you must creep and deceive me to get anything from me.

'You have wounded me, and for that, and your brazen lies - not for the theft of my fire, which is free for all who would take it - I will punish you. You want fire? I will give you fire. I give you love, and I give it to you *cursed*. Henceforth, you will know love, and yearn for it. You, who were unaware that being part god, you possess a soul, will now desire the completion of your soul. Your soul will now burn you as mine burns within you. You will desire, and never be filled. You will want pleasure, and it will not complete you; you will want pain, and hate yourself for it, and still it will not complete you because it is, after all, only another sensation. Your earthly half will long for feeling, your divine half for worship, and the two urges will war within you and torment you. You will pass this curse on to your children. Will you yet love me? Will you long for me with hopeless hunger, the way I have longed for you? That I cannot control, for love will give you independence, but the high wall of unknowing will steal peace from you. Thus I am avenged.

'Cadwal and Aron! Do not think you can escape this curse! You have been accomplices. You, too, shall therefore know what it is to love. Your baser natures will war with your souls. Desire will inflict jealousy on you, because your sublime souls will be tainted with earthly need. You will want to possess that which you love. You will fight, even kill, to that end, and you will not even be able to tell whether you fight for love or merely for want. You will be divorced from the female half of your species by your desire; desire will choke what brotherly love you might have shared. The same will occur when you turn to each other for fulfillment, or when woman seeks her soul in another woman's embrace: even that love will not be free of the curse. Love will turn to estrangement, being always tempered with need. Until you can come to terms with need, you will never regain your souls. You will, instead, become needier yet. Your divine blood will be a plague, a curse. It is no longer a gift.

'The fire? Oh, you can keep that. As I have said, it is free to all. It is but a toy. I will not take it from you - believe me, you will need it to light the darkness, even though you will come to see its burning, too, as a curse.'

"And then he was gone.

"And so the two-legged ones knew love; and you are all familiar with how Cadwal slew Aron for want of Lily and thus became the sole father of the human species. You have heard the mystery. I do not understand it. I comprehend romance no more than I comprehend tame fire or the art of cooking dead flesh; the only building that I understand is the building of nests. Yet this is the story as it has been passed down, and it is true that every male with two legs is of Cadwal, and every female with two legs is of Lily. These creatures are compelled to carry the curse from generation to generation, to live out their myths as they multiply."

The rook ceased. And I saw that there could indeed be two ways to end this parliament: the rook could go free, or it could be pecked to death, its story forever silenced.

Sometime later, my guide took me once again through the forest, and left me at the gate of horn.

Where I awoke; and I resolved, in his words, to "read something to improve myself, therefore I shall contrive reading all the more." Perhaps Dante might have been a better guide - I would have liked to have asked him some questions about his divine *eros* for Beatrice. However, of some of the mysteries it is not permitted to speak; you merely experience them, or you don't. I know this. I'm a melancholiac with odd fancies that I have a hard time committing to paper. I wonder if I should have recorded this at all, but if the rook was at all true in his words, then I, as Lily's child, should be well accustomed to stealing fire and doing the forbidden. Do forbidden stories emerge into the morning without that taint of blood, I wonder? Or are they always divine and incomprehensible?

THE MAGUS

ANCILLA

CHAPTER I

ANCILLA EXCERPT: THE MAGUS

In Morsels, *I'm including two early chapters from my novel,* Ancilla. *The two chapters introduce my characters and subject material without providing plot spoilers.*

Here is the first chapter in which the protagonist's main love interest appears. It comes after the world's longest prologue.

The man standing next to me in the Classic Literature section of the bookstore has interesting taste. Surreptitiously, I'll look up every now and then to see what else is in his stack of books; I can't see all the titles, but from what I can tell, it's an eclectic mix of occult philosophy, poetry, history, and something I can't quite make out. Some kind of fiction, maybe. Given the section we're both browsing, that seems to be a reasonable assumption to make.

He's also very good-looking, for an older man. Hair dark sable, with strands of silver – a shade of brown so dark that it's almost black. On second glance, maybe it *is* black. I can't tell in this lighting. Nice wool dress trousers, silk shirt, both slightly rumpled, both in dark hues. Slender – unusually so – I suspect he has muscle, but of the wiry sort. Pale skin, a bit on the olive side. Almost my height, so he's tall. I'd say he's probably about six feet one or so, maybe six-two.

There's something compelling about his hands, although I can't for the life of me say exactly what. Maybe it's because of the way they're held still, but seem full of pent-up energy. Maybe it's the fascinating way they're gnarled and lined. I look at his hands and think of the grove of birches that was on the lawn in front of my college library.

He's interesting.

His books look interesting, too.

Heck with it.

"You buy books the way I do – in bulk," I say to him. "What have you got so far?" It's been a long while since I've been able to buy my books rather than just read them in the store while soaking in the bookstore ambiance, but I don't feel like talking about that.

Without a word, he holds out his books for me to see. Books on the Golden Dawn; the complete poems of William Butler Yeats – all right, I saw those earlier. A rather outdated text on the supposed religion of the Etruscans written by Charles Godfrey Leland. Saw that. Then I see the titles I didn't catch earlier. An issue of *Gnosis*. An issue of *Yellow Silk*. Nice. Umberto Eco's *Semiotics and the Philosophy of Language*. Jung's *Red Book*. Some paperback with a plain yellow cover and the title in understated black lettering; the author appears to be French. So does the book's title, which means whatever the book is he's reading, it's in the original French, unless it was written in English, in which case he's reading a French translation for whatever reason. The first scenario seems the more plausible one. Hmm. *Histoire* translates as "story," if I remember correctly from my very rusty lower-school French classes. It's fiction. Other than that, I've no idea what it is, and I can't puzzle it out.

At the bottom of his pile are a couple of Julia Child cookbooks.

"You cook?"

"It's one of my hobbies."

He has an accent. I can't place it, though. His voice is too quiet. The only thing I can determine is that it's not Midwestern, so he's possibly not from around here.

I want to hear him talk more. It's not just that I'm hoping I might be able to place the accent if I listen to it more. It's also the fact that his hushed voice is warm and velvety and seductive. It needs to be on a recording. (Ideally, that recording would be a romance novel).

Cute. Unusual voice. Multilingual. Broad taste in reading, including some stuff I've heard of or read, and some stuff I've never heard of that looks like I might want to hear of it at some point in the indefinite near future... and he cooks? *Very* interesting.

"Leland's not considered very reliable," I remark. "He had a pronounced tendency to embellish or to just make things up. His writings are classics, as far as the Western mystery tradition is concerned, but they're not good primary resources for mythological or anthropological research."

I'm so good at making polite small talk that I amaze myself.

"True. Of course, Aleister Crowley made up more than half of what he wrote, but he's a classic in his own way, as well." He's so quiet. Shy, or just reserved? I can't tell.

"Haven't read him yet. He's on my get-around-to list, though."

Silence.

"You like poetry?"

"Yes. Although I'm also reading Yeats as part of my study of the philosophy of the Order of the Golden Dawn."

"Oh."

More silence.

"Where did you find the magazines and the books? I've never seen these in the New Age section." His selections look way too esoteric for a little shopping mall bookstore like this one.

"I put them on order."

Our hands brush as I hand him back his books.

I think I just made him blush.

Shy. Definitely shy.

I've spotted him again. Funny how I'd never noticed him here before, given how I practically live in the downtown library when I'm not selling magazines –

a part-time telemarketing job that I hate, because no matter how good I am at it, I'm always afraid one bad week will get me fired. Also, faking being an outgoing "people person" is exhausting, especially since they have me assigned to a day shift right now, which means I also have to fake being a "morning person," and no amount of free coffee seems to completely do the trick for that.

It could be I've never spotted him here because I don't usually use the reference section. Most of what I read is in circulation even when it's not fiction. Today, though, I'm looking for books and journals on archaeology related to the Trojan War. Rereading Lattimore's translation of the *Iliad* made me curious, and of course, I couldn't let the subject rest once it had lodged itself in my mind (well, reading it completely for the first time, really; like many books I was assigned for courses, while I was taking the honors tutorial on Bronze Age Greece I couldn't bring myself to read the assigned material from cover to cover, and only skimmed it, only to rediscover it later when I had more time on my hands and when the reading was not compulsory, and part of a heavy course load that competed with several other classes, all of which had their own homework). Translations of the *Iliad* and the *Odyssey* are in circulation, of course, as are some books on ancient history, including a couple that focus exclusively on the Trojan War, but aside from a coffee table book by Michael Grant that seems to be the book form of a PBS miniseries, there's nothing on archaeology in circulation. So now I'm here.

He's one of the reference librarians.

I walk up to the desk. "I don't know how to find the journals Manfred Korfmann published his findings in. Could you help me, please?"

"I can check the print index. You'll have better luck finding those in the university library, though. What we have on classical civilization and archaeology is extremely basic. If you like, we could order some materials through interlibrary loan… But I think you should use the classical collection at the university library. It's well-stocked, plus they currently have an exhibition of documents on loan from the Blegen Center archives, including excavation records from the Palace of

Nestor and some of Carl Blegen's original papers. They also have some first-edition Schliemanns. You'd love it."

And then his face lights up.

"*You again!*"

"Me again."

We act quietly flustered at each other, including some obligatory awkward conversational pauses.

Finally, I blurt out, "Want to go out on a date with me?"

Another awkward pause.

He smiles. "All right. Yes."

This more than makes up for my not having found the journals I was looking for.

We sat in the cloud club section of the university auditorium for a traveling repertory company's performance of *Die Zauberflöte*. What we miss in a close-up view we gain in good acoustics, which is just as well because neither a telemarketer nor a librarian can easily afford the more expensive seats. This, I think, had to have been as perfect a first date as one could get. A bonus is that I have established that he likes opera. Most of my acquaintances think my love of opera is insane, or at least a sign of some deeper character disturbance.

"I thought Monostatos was a bit much. So was the Queen of the Night, for that matter."

"You should have seen the libretto before Mozart edited it," he replies.

"It was *worse*? How could you get much worse than an evil, lustful Moor saying his blackness made him ugly, so he wanted to rape and kidnap the pretty white girl who wouldn't be interested in an ugly guy like him, which sounds like the plot of *Birth of a Nation* only too early and wrong setting, and a malicious queen with too much power telling her daughter that she'll disown her if she doesn't subjugate the hero, and, oh, yeah, an occult brotherhood admonishing the hero and his sidekick to avoid women if they want to be enlightened?"

"It was worse. Rather in the same way *The Taming of the Shrew* was far more misogynistic before Shakespeare wrote his own version of the play, and *The Merchant of Venice* was even more anti-Semitic when it was *Il Pecorone*."

"Oh, well, at least the music was good," I say with a sigh as we climb the stairs to his apartment. I like the street his apartment building is on. It's a quiet residential cul-de-sac on the west side of town, without many other houses or other buildings on it. His section of the street is right across from a cemetery, and there are lots of trees, so the overall effect is almost park-like.

"That it was." He unlocks the door and lets me in.

I am now perched on his couch, drinking peppermint tea and feeling the unseasonably warm, cherry blossom-scented breeze that blows through the open window. I take in details of his apartment while he bustles in the kitchen – I'm failing dismally to be subtle about it, but he's in the kitchen, so that's all right, I guess. The living room decorations consist of bookshelves. All the shelves are used for books. Some shelves are double stacked, including all the shelves on a bookcase that appears to be dedicated to science fiction and fantasy trade paperbacks. I wonder if he would loan out his books if I asked nicely.

There's a magazine called *Prometheus*, lying on top of the issue of *Gnosis* and the issue of *Yellow Silk*. It seems to be a literary magazine of some kind. It looks interesting.

I pick it up off the table – which is really an ornately carved chest – and flip it open at random.

On the left page is a poem. On the right is an exquisitely rendered drawing of a bound and gagged woman. The placement of the ropes is elaborate enough that it makes me squint and turn my head, trying to figure out how everything was set up. In real life, it would be a sculpture with rope. My eyes flick left; the poem – which is beautifully written – seems to go along with the art. As I turn the pages, I notice a distinct and recurring theme to them.

Of course, it would be just this moment that he emerges from the kitchen carrying a tray of freshly baked chocolate chip cookies.

The awkward silence between us this time is very awkward indeed.

"Very artistically done," I say at last. No, I am not blushing. And I'm not stammering. That is not a stammer. Not at all.

He puts the tray of cookies down on a side table. In a quiet and careful voice, he replies, "That's the literary journal of the oldest BDSM society in North America."

"Oh."

There's a literary journal?

"Have you read the poetry of Swinburne?" I finally ask. "Some of his poems combined eroticism and pain."

"I'm quite fond of Swinburne," he replies.

"Same here," I murmur, willing my mug of tea to calm my hands, which are shaking. "It's amazing the things you can find in libraries."

My eyes lift and wander back to his shelves. Aside from the bookcase devoted to speculative fiction, there is also a stack of history and archaeology books – heavy on prehistory, early Near Eastern and Egyptian history, and classical Greece and Rome – and two cases contain texts on philosophy and comparative religion. A tall case in the corner nearest the couch is crammed with occult lore of various backgrounds.

One shelf at eye level has several books on Tantra and ceremonial sex magick. It also has a couple of non-occult-related texts relating to different activities also starting with the letters "S" and "M," which, while not mystical and esoteric, are nevertheless fairly mysterious, at least to me.

"You filed them with your occult books?"

"Yes."

Silence again. These silences are getting painfully tense.

I swallow past the dryness in my throat. "Why?"

"Because they go together. It's not unheard of; for instance, Gerald Gardner and Aleister Crowley were both notorious for it, each in their own way. Also, if you get into the histories and philosophies of various parts of Asia, you'll find a strong note of mystical asceticism."

"And you?" Stupid voice. Stop croaking.

"I follow an established Western mystery tradition, but there are some things that I make up as I go along."

I look down as I sip my peppermint tea. It's gone cold.

The quiet of the room descends again. My heart rattles against my chest. I breathe deeply and try to think about nothing, to let my feelings flow past and away, as they do when I sit *zazen*. I listen to myself breathe. I make my breathing slow and calm until the quiet of the room no longer hurts.

I'm extremely surprised that my reaction is so violent. There really is no reason for me to be shaken by the mere mention of sexual kinks in a conversation, or by their portrayal in written and visual art. It's not like I only just now found out such things existed. Of course, the man whose living room couch I am sitting on seems rather more involved in such matters than any other love interest I've had so far. No doubt that has something to do with it, although it once again raises the question of why I am trembling from nervous excitement. Why be nervous? That's silly...

Oh.

Not quite meeting me in the eyes, he asks in a small voice, "Do you still find me attractive?"

I put down the tea and rise from the couch. I walk over to where he is standing, put his face between my hands, and pull him close to me until his lips are touching mine.

"Yes," I whisper against his mouth, and as he reaches for me and encircles me with his arms, the room's silence becomes a heat I can almost touch.

I turned twenty-one today. We didn't have enough money to go out to eat, and there were not enough ingredients in the larder to bake any kind of dessert from scratch, so we are sharing some packaged cupcakes we got from a convenience store in lieu of traditional birthday cake.

We've been seeing each other for several weeks now. I hesitate to call it "dating," or to call him my "boyfriend," because he's twice my age, and "dating" and "boyfriends" seem inappropriately adolescent as ways to describe an affair with him – and it is an affair. We aren't boyfriend and girlfriend, going steady and making plans to attend the prom. We're lovers.

He gave me a birthday present: a rare used hardback copy of the poems of Emily Dickinson. It's an antique first edition – maybe not of the poems themselves, but certainly of that particular anthology, which was printed in the very early part of this century. And it's in mint condition. This is probably the reason my "birthday cake" consists of plastic-wrapped snack food. I'll take the book over cake any day, though, especially when part of my present involves his reading aloud to me.

Wild nights, wild nights,
were I with thee,
Wild nights should be
our luxury –

He punctuates the verses with kisses: my forehead, my cheeks, my hair, my neck. My lips. My lips are burning under his. He has such soft, warm lips, to take my breath away.

Futile the winds
to the heart in port –
Done with the compass,
done with the chart –

Time to screw my courage to the sticking point.

I lean back into his embrace, and interrupt him by whispering in his ear, "Master, teach me."

His breath stops, and I feel his body suddenly become as tense as a bowstring. Any more tense and he'll be jumping out of his skin.

"*What?*"

"I know what you want. And I know what I want. Master, teach me."

He groans quietly and closes his eyes. He's closing them against himself, I think. That can't be very effective.

"You don't know what you're asking."

"I ransacked your personal library on our last few dates, remember? Then there was that little game of Twenty Questions we played last night. Good heavens. I know what I'm asking."

"Do you have any idea what kind of effect you're having on me?"

"Yes. Yes, I do. I know because I can see you. Silly. I can reach out and feel you, too, where you're threatening to burst out of your pants. Master, teach me. I want to apprentice myself."

I can feel him trembling. Am I trembling too? I must be. My voice is. But all I feel is him.

"Is this something you really want, or do you just want to learn how to be a dominant?" Shaking. God, he's shaking. His raw need rips through me. "You did mention your former girlfriend wanting you to play the dominant. I can advise you without actually asking anything of you if that's the case. Or is this about that conversation we had a while back about studying magic –"

"If I only wanted advice, I'd ask for advice. I don't just want advice. I want *you*. Master, teach me." I take a deep breath.

Silence falls.

"I want that very badly," he says at last.

"I'm yours for the taking. Please. Take me."

The room is still. Too still. The very air is holding its breath.

"Please."

The only one trembling now is me.

He seizes my wrists in one of his hands and pins them to the futon, behind my head. My nose decides now, of all times, to itch, and I try to scratch it, but of course, I can't, because he's pinning me down. I can't get loose. I had no idea he had this much strength. He's only slightly built, but he has me caught. He's unbuttoning me with his other hand, freeing my breasts, and he squeezes my nipple until it is hard, and I moan with desire, arching against him, nearly lifting him off the futon with me as I do so.

"We need to negotiate. Is there anything you absolutely do not want to do?"

"I don't know."

"Of course. Rather silly of me to ask, if you don't know what my specific quirks might be. I probably have you at something of a disadvantage, as well." He smiles. "Should I stop?"

"Oh, no. Please don't stop..."

He's teasing my nipple with his fingers, kissing and nibbling my neck, and licking around my ear in slow, careful circles, making me cry out and writhe and buck up against him. I am made of fire and need. Such little things – of course, he's kissed me and used his fingers to pleasure me before, and done other things as well, leading to the usual denouement, but somehow it was never like this. What is this? Being pinned down makes everything different? That doesn't make sense; I've been pinned down in martial arts, many times, and never responded this wildly, not even when it turned me on. His personality, maybe? Something he's doing? I am being consumed. I had no idea it would feel this way. So delirious. Oh, so beautiful.

Raggedly, he asks, "What do you dream about doing?"

That's harder to answer than it might initially sound. The things he's doing to me almost make me forget how to speak; I just want to moan. I find it oddly comforting that he's struggling to keep his composure as well. Let us both be consumed by the same fire. "Um. I've never actually been tied up before, myself, although my last girlfriend had me tie her up once. The end result was a bit awkward. I told you about that. I saw a riding crop in a novelty store in the mall that looked really interesting. I get turned on thinking about Vulcan mind melds."

He stares at me incredulously. "Vulcan mind melds?"

"They're romantic."

"Hmm. Unfortunately, I don't think I can help you out with the Vulcan mind meld thing." He takes his free hand, wraps it around my jaw, and presses his mouth to mine. Now my mouth is as trapped as my arms are; he opens me and devours me with his tongue. Meanwhile, his body is still pressing itself on mine, grinding into mine. He's hard – incredibly so. It feels good. I start to moan.

"First lesson: you do not speak until I give you leave. You do not cry out. You do not moan."

Rats.

"Noise releases energy; I want you to keep your energy inside until I ask for it." He takes his hand off my jaw and, moving aside slightly, reaches down under my leggings and underwear to rub his fingers against me. I'm soaked. I almost whimper, but I have to stay quiet. Not being able to make noise hurts. I feel my hips rocking of their own accord.

"Be still."

Now *that* was not even remotely fair.

His fingers continue to play with my nether lips as he works off my clothes, rubbing wet cotton back and forth against my genitals as he pulls my panties down. I can't move. I can't moan. I gasp desperately on the edge of orgasm.

"Open your legs."

I do my best to comply. It's not difficult; I am burning up with my own need. At some point he must have removed some of his own garments; I never even noticed, and for some reason, I find that eerily disorienting.

He still has me by the wrists.

"Wider."

No, no, I can't scream when he enters me, I can't. I can't move. I have to contain this. I bite my lip, trying not to make noise.

His mouth on my mouth, his lips on my lips. "Mine," he gasps. His free hand is in my hair, holding me fast. "Mine, now. Mine." Suddenly he yanks me back, hard, and I feel his teeth wrap around my exposed throat. Biting. He moves down, down all along my neck, covering me with bites, seizing my skin, and pulling on it as if he could suck my soul from out of my flesh.

"*Mine.*"

Driving into me, violently; the futon is soaked with the juices of my desire, the sweat pouring from me as I strain to avoid crying out in ecstasy, avoid wrapping my legs around him to move things to my own pace. Too much –

He bends down and murmurs into my ear, "I am going to kiss you again. When you need to scream, scream into my mouth. Give your scream to me."

His voice is shaking.

It doesn't take me long; within seconds, I am screaming. I am also writhing, bucking, thrusting madly against him as my orgasm overwhelms both of us.

"I need to grab a couple of things. Wait right there, please. Don't move."

Right. I'm not going anywhere.

He is only gone for a couple of moments – it's not exactly a large apartment – and when he returns, he has some unfamiliar items in his hands. They're black and leathery. I stare in fascination; my imaginary idea of being "tied up" has so far been limited to things like scarves and curtain ropes, because those things are a normal part of my daily life, whereas articles made of black-dyed leather are not. The smell of the leather is intoxicating. It's not a shoe store smell at all. It's sharper. It's almost narcotic. It goes up into my nostrils when I breathe, down through my lungs, and out places to which I never expected lungs to have any connection.

"Hold out your wrists."

I hold them out obligingly. I want to see what these things are and how they work.

They're a pair of leather manacles, cushioned and lined with some kind of velvety soft fabric, adjusted with holes and buckles, shiny silvery things that look as attractive to my perverted magpie eyes as the leather itself. He uses the tightest setting.

Then he puts my wrists over my head and affixes them to something that goes click. It appears to be a clip, attached to a chain, attached to an eye bolt screwed into the futon frame. I had no idea that it was even there. How interesting.

"Your wrists are almost too thin for these to properly restrain you." He looks down at me with a concerned expression. "I've always noticed you were slender, of course, but goodness, that's thin. Are you getting enough to eat?"

"Yes."

"Hmm."

The other black, leathery thing is a riding crop.

"Riding crops are very versatile," he says, as he settles into a kneeling position and picks up the crop. "You'll want to have one of your own eventually. The one you saw in the mall – if it was the same store I'm thinking of – was cheap and shoddy and would not have been good for much other than show; you'll want something a little more high-end if you want to use it as a whip. The cheap version you saw will also be hard to clean because it's braided suede, and whatever soap or other cleaner you use on it will tend to get lodged in the braided parts – another strike against it."

My voice is an octave higher than normal when I ask, "So, what do you do with it?" I hadn't intended on that. Oops.

Sangfroid apparently isn't one of my more reliable virtues when I'm facing a riding crop.

"Attend." He takes the handled end and thrusts it gently under my chin, forcing my head back. "Many people find this a little intimidating, especially when they are immobilized or otherwise helpless, possibly because of the threat of the riding crop itself being used."

"Um. Yes, I can see that."

"Your voice is shaking. Did you know that? By the way, I remind you that you are to be silent and still until I give you leave when you are receiving lessons. From now on, be quiet, please. Another use for the riding crop: you can gently stroke a slave's nerve endings to provoke arousal. If you are knowledgeable of such things as pressure points and nerve paths, the effect can be quite explosive. Different people, of course, can have different sensitive spots. I haven't had a chance to find all of yours yet; in time, I imagine I will."

Do I get to return the favor? I wonder. Practice makes perfect, after all... The possibility intrigues me. Then thought ceases as he pushes the flap of the crop gently behind my ear and trails it along my jawline, down to my collarbone. Then down and around my breasts, circling my nipples, first one, then the other. Then back again. Up and down, until he strokes my cheek with the shaft and places its length against my lips. There it rests. Eventually, I figure out that I'm supposed to kiss it, so I press my lips against the leather, imagining that I am kissing not an inanimate object, but flesh. The crop is an extension of my lover now, and I kiss it fervently.

"Good," he says, and once again the shaft moves along my cheek until the flap is again stroking my skin, moving down to trace the outlines of my breasts, small circles that spiral in until he is rubbing my nipples back and forth with the leather. He gives my left one a light smack. I gasp and force myself to hold still. I want to groan; I want to sway into the motion of the strokes. But that is forbidden to me.

He trails the flap down my abdomen slowly until it is hovering between my legs, stroking my clitoris, rubbing up against my labia with the shaft end, back and forth in a massaging motion until I feel a cry building at the bottom of my throat, escaping my mouth as a faint, high-pitched keening despite my best efforts to remain silent. He taps me on my clit, and I gulp. It wasn't even a very hard tap, it didn't hurt me at all, and yet suddenly I am terrified.

"Shh, now," he murmurs, leaning down to touch my cheek. "I've got you. Are you all right? You may nod or shake your head."

I nod.

"Is this still what you want?" He caresses my face with his free hand.

I nod again.

He leans over, covers my lips with his, my body with his body, and my world becomes stable again. It had been shaking, or I had been shaking, but I hadn't even fully noticed until I felt his flesh against mine, reassuring me with its warmth. I relax into him as he grounds me with kisses and heat.

Don't stop. Please, don't stop.

"I'm here," he says, and he buries me under his weight. His lips are so soft, his breath so delicious. We sigh into each other as our tongues duel.

When he pulls away, I notice he is slightly breathless. I, on the other hand, am oddly full of energy.

"Let us continue. Various parts of the riding crop can be used on the genitals, in various ways, depending on whether your slave is male or female, and on whether that person is into pain. Not all submissives have a masochistic streak; not all dominants are sadists. If your objective is to produce pleasure that does not involve pain, you might try using the handle for penetration... Hold still, please. And I remind you again, do not make any noise. I want you to keep your sounds, and energy, inside." He would have to illustrate that one. "Until I say otherwise." Of course, he tells me this as he proceeds to do everything possible to make me writhe and cry out.

Pressure, little nudges. Oh, God.

It's very difficult to keep still and silent when the head of his riding crop is pushing at some of my more sensitive areas. I glare at him. So far, that's still acceptable.

"Consider this honing your willpower; you'll need it when you're the dominant. Willpower is important when your submissive asks you to stop doing something, and you don't want to stop, but have to stop anyway. That is what the social contract demands. Scene etiquette requires consent, even when you are perpetuating the illusion of non-consent. Speaking of which, since many submissives like to have you pretend that they are being forced to submit, they may scream 'no,' or 'stop,' or 'mercy,' or something like that, without meaning it literally, which is one reason why safewords are important. A safeword is a word that all parties agree on that means 'I really do mean stop.' The other major reason safewords get used is that dominants are as human as the next person and are as likely as anyone else to get carried away in the heat of the moment if things get very intense; a safeword sounds a bit incongruous and is more likely than 'no' or 'stop' to get an impassioned dominant's attention and halt the activity, should that be necessary. What would you like to be yours? You have leave to answer."

I think. I try to think, anyway. Martial arts. "*Mate,*" I reply, a bit unsteadily, partly because what he's still doing with the head of the riding crop (good grief, he never even paused. *Not once*) is nothing I want to associate with the word "stop."

"That would work well," he muses. "I studied *aikido* some years ago, also *ninjutsu* and a couple of other martial arts; hearing the word *mate* would make me stop automatically. It's almost Pavlovian. When not given leave to speak or make noise, meanwhile, please pound three times with your fist, or flex your hand three times, or grunt three times in succession. I will be watching for it. When you are in a position of power over someone, you should do the same. It does not have to be the three thumps or grunts, of course; it can be anything the two of you agree on. Are you getting all that?"

I nod yes.

The handle of the crop continues to push against me with an impatient sort of stiffness and weight. I gasp, choking on the screams of pleasure I'm holding inside. So close.

"Good. Roll over."

He hasn't moved the head of the riding crop yet. It's still shoved inside me. Rolling over proves interesting; the fact that I can't use my arms doesn't help much, either. I hope I look cute when I'm flopping around like a fish and humping myself on the head of a crop.

Unfortunately, he stops what he's doing before I can come again and pulls the crop handle out. The loop of the wrist strap trails, teasing me, and brushes my thigh on its way out, leaving me covered with the evidence of my need.

The near edge of orgasm hurts me like a knife.

"There are two other standard uses for a riding crop," he says, wiping the crop handle off with his shirt tail. "One is rather obvious. And today happens to be your birthday. You're twenty-one today, yes? Let's round it up to thirty and give you a few to grow on. It builds character. Would you like that?"

"I don't know. Maybe. There's only one way to find out."

"Yes, that's very true."

He slowly trails the tip of the riding crop down my back until it reaches my buttocks, caressing me with the shaft in slow circles until the crop rests in perfect alignment with what I suspect is the only part of my posterior to have anything resembling curves.

He lets it hover there for one long moment before he lays into me.

I don't scream. I don't grunt, flex my hand, or tap out, either.

He lies on top of my back. It doesn't hurt as much as it could. Part of this might be distraction; his hand is underneath me, working the wet spot between my legs. It might also be more accurate to say that yes, it does rather hurt to have him draping himself on top of my backside, given my injuries, which are not major but are just raw enough to sting, but what he's doing to me is distracting enough that I don't really care that it stings to have him lying on top of welts.

And no, I still can't make noise.

He has hardened again. I suppose that shouldn't come as a surprise.

"I will not repeat the experience if you didn't enjoy it; you did say, however, that you were interested in riding crops. Was that... welcome? Or was it too much?" He has that shy sound in his voice again. I think I like it at least as much as the steel that came out tonight. "You have leave to speak."

I smile, although he probably can't see me do it. "Oh, don't worry. It was welcome."

"The other standard use for a riding crop is as a gag," he says as he rises from his position on my back. "Open your mouth. Good. Bite down."

Now he's gagging me? Why not before? Oh, right. Energy.

"Do not make noise. You may, however, move. Lift, please."

He slips a pillow underneath my hips as I rest my weight on my elbows and knees to raise myself. Then he leans down to whisper in my ear, and I feel his hand slide between my legs. God, I'm gushing.

"Ride my fingers."

He has them inside me now – I'm not sure how many – more than two, less than five – I think. Maybe. Maybe he does have all five of them in there. I can feel his knuckles against the bones of my pelvis. Pressure, fullness, my nerves stretched like tightrope. One of his fingers gently massages my clitoris. His thumb? Maybe. No, that's not anatomically possible, is it? I can't tell. For all I know, he might be using both hands. I'm wet enough that the sensation of being stuffed gives me no discomfort, only pleasure. I rock, I rock, and I am drowned in wave after wave of orgasm. Dear God, keep doing that, whatever it is. I'll ask you what and how later. Not now. Oh.

Want to scream. Can't.

Arching back. Biting down; pushing hard against the hand inside me. So good, I want this forever. I don't want it to end. Ever.

When my body relaxes, and I collapse in a heap on the pillow, he says, "Open your legs again. You closed them."

I was expecting him to immediately slide inside me and take me the way he did before, but instead, I feel his fingers, which are still covered with the juice of my orgasms, sliding up into the smaller orifice between my buttocks. Lubricating me. I hope he's gentle. The last time I tried this with a boyfriend, it was somewhat awkward and painful. What he's doing with his fingers is certainly nice enough. It almost seems a shame for him to stop.

When he slides into me, I find myself biting down on the riding crop, but not because of any kind of pain. He's very good at what he's doing. Astonishingly good. I didn't know it could feel *this* pleasurable. I want so badly to make noise. To move.

Maybe he won't notice if I twitch my hips against him just a little.

Ever so slightly, he groans.

I wonder if I can also get away with making a few small noises. Just little moans. Surely little moans would be all right?

Gasping, he reaches for me with his other hand, the one he did not use to lubricate me, and I do my best to entwine my fingers around his.

Then he shudders and lets out a loud sigh as he spends himself, collapsing on top of me.

His weight is warm and good. Breath hot against my skin. Kisses on my neck and cheeks; he can't quite reach my lips.

"Happy birthday," he says.

He leans in to kiss me on the cheek; I rub my nose against the pillow, because I'm itching again, and his kiss lands on my ear.

"I presume I can talk now?"

I hear him smiling, although I can't see it from this position. "Yes."

"My wrists are starting to get uncomfortable. Could you please let me out, now?"

"Oh. Of course. Sorry." He does.

It occurs to me that I also desperately need to use the bathroom, both to empty my bladder and to clean off; I stumble in that direction, knees wobbly from exhaustion and pleasure, and when I return, it's his turn to use the various facilities.

I burrow myself into his arms when he lies back down beside me.

"Was that what you were looking for?"

"It was what was necessary. I look forward to learning more. That, and... yes. Yes, it was." I pause, not quite sure how to phrase all the words and feelings that are rolling in me like large waves. "Thank you, Master." That wasn't coached. It did, however, seem the polite thing to say.

"Hold me," he whispers. "Hold me."

Rowing in Heaven, ah, the sea; might I but moor tonight in thee.

ANCILLA EXCERPT: MALKUTH

This is the second excerpt from my novel. I chose it because it provides a good introduction to the magickal and spiritual system that is the backbone of Ancilla, because it doesn't really spoil any plot, and last but not least, because it's spicy.

If you liked the two passages you just read, the novel is available in both print and electronic editions from Amazon and other booksellers.

The blinds are down, and the curtains drawn over the windows, so that neighbors and casual passers-by will not get an eyeful. We are in the living room because this is the room that has the most open floor space. It's also where he keeps his altar and his ritual supplies. They store easily enough when not in use; he keeps most of them in the carved ornamental chest that doubles as a coffee table and an altar. Tonight, he has some of the supplies laid out on top of it. A chalice filled with water; a dish with salt in it; a long, slender dagger made of what appears to be bronze; two lit candles; a long wooden rod of some kind.

Some of the supplies have already been used to cast the circle around us. Tonight, the circle is designated as a space for lessons.

Shadows flicker and dance on the walls from the candlelight. There is no other light, although there are enough candles that either one of us could read a book without straining our eyes. Just.

"You are, I believe, familiar with these concepts already," he says, "but reviewing them will be helpful. We will work together better in a cast circle if our perspectives, and thus our energies, are in absolute synchrony. Attend."

I am naked and sitting straight-backed on my knees in the classic student posture that I had been using for years to practice Zen meditation. There isn't much difference between meditating and actively listening to *Magister* in that regard (that being the formal title we have settled on; it was also decided that the best description of my role, incorporating all aspects as an apprentice, student, temple servant, and sexual submissive, would not be *discipula* but the more general term *ancilla*). Except, of course, I never sat *zazen* while nude.

He is also nude tonight. This has not always been the case – the act of wearing clothes when one's student or servant is naked carries its own semiotic power, and so far, when he's taken me into his bedroom for instruction, he's made it a practice to keep me naked and himself at least somewhat clothed – but tonight we are going to do magickal work, and there is raw honesty in nudity. This, too, is a departure from his usual habit; he usually does his magickal work while wearing ritual clothing. Tonight, however, he is bringing me into the circle formally for the first time. Tonight, this one time, therefore, we are both in the world as we originally entered it.

"The first element I intend to work with is Air, which is associated with the east and the light of dawn; with ideas, beginnings, and the mind. Before we act, we think. In the beginning, there is *Logos*." He takes the bronze dagger from the altar. "My tradition uses a dagger to represent Air. Most of the Western mystery traditions use a blade of some kind. High ceremonial magick uses a very specific kind of wand for Air, and a sword for Fire, perhaps because trees, which provide wood for wands and staves, get blown around in the wind, and blades, meanwhile, are forged in fire; but I think the symbolism in my own tradition makes just as much sense. Wood can be set on fire, and the metal of a blade can conduct heat or cold depending on the temperature of the air, and it cuts through the air on the way to its destination. Furthermore, the metal blade is hard and keen, as is the focused will. Blades are therefore Air. That is how I learned magick, and that is how I am used to doing things."

He thrusts the tip of the dagger against the soft, hollow spot of flesh just under my chin. Reflexively, I start to look down.

"I wouldn't," he says mildly. "It's extremely sharp. Look up instead."

I look up.

"It would be better to run onto this blade than to cast or use the circle in fear," he intones. I recognize the phrase from one of my independent readings in the occult. This isn't the exact phrase; he's using a variation. I can't remember which tradition makes use of it. Possibly my memory lapse is due to the sharp tip of a dagger biting into my flesh. "How do you serve? You may speak."

Think. "In perfect love and perfect trust," I reply, my voice mostly managing to avoid rising into the squeak range.

"Good focus. That was what I was looking for." He pauses. "Also, the trust, of course. Rise."

I don't really have a choice in the matter; the blade is pushing up hard against me, lifting me. If I don't rise with it, I'm going to get a worse cut than the minor, tickling nick I gave myself while trying to look down when I should have been looking up. I rise, and follow him slowly across the room, led by knifepoint.

Candlelit shadows jump crazily in our wake.

He's led me to the couch. "Stand," he says, "and bend over, supporting yourself on the back of the couch. Arms out. Good."

I knew this was coming.

"The next element is Fire, which I have reason to believe is your primary element, which means your training will be rather more difficult than it might be were you primarily of Air, Water, or Earth. It's not an easy or gentle element to work with. It represents the southern direction, desire, passion, action, heat, raw energy, and courage; if Air is the will, Fire is the imperative. You will recall that I talked about it being represented by wands, although a branch of Western ceremonial magick uses a sword instead. Either way, the meaning conveyed by the symbolic instrument is the same. I have a staff that I use in my solitary rituals, one I constructed and painted myself, which is standing in the corner of the room, but it isn't appropriate for what we will do here." From the corner of my eye, I see him taking the rod from the altar. I turn my head to get a better look at it. It's a long pale slender stick, has a red handle, and appears to be about three feet in length. "I've never used this particular wand before, for ritual use or for anything else. Nor will I after our tutoring sessions end. It will be yours, and you will most certainly have earned it. I remind you that you do not have leave to cry out, nor do you have leave to move from your position until I say otherwise. This tool is a little harder, and a little harder to bear, than others we've worked with so far. I thought it best to warn you. Brace yourself."

I feel the slight breeze before I hear the whooshing sound of the cane, and then fire lands across my thighs. I gasp. It's all I can do to keep from yelling, and while I don't move out of position, I flinch hard.

"Courage," he says, and then the blows rain down.

I can't scream. I can't jerk away or dance in place. But I can cry; he hasn't said anything about that, and eventually, despite my efforts to stifle them, sobs come up my throat, and I am choking on them, and tears are pouring out of me in torrents.

It stops. In the sudden quiet, I notice that I am shaking and covered with sweat; I wonder how long I have been this way. I feel him coming up behind me, and then his arms are around me and he has his hands on my sweating breasts and body; he kisses me on the neck, and as I start to melt into him, his kisses turn to nips and then the deep, possessive bites I love, making me gasp. His hand reaches down between my legs. It's harder not to moan than it was to avoid screaming.

At least he seems to be in a similar state. I can feel his erection poking me in the back.

"Courage," he whispers, and pulls away just as I am on the verge of orgasm.

I hear him picking up the cane again.

"Have courage," he says, a little more loudly, and it is all I can do to obey.

I am collapsed on the couch, unable to move. I haven't been secured. There is no need. I am too exhausted, and in too much hurt, to even think of getting up.

My nerves are on fire.

Perhaps that was the point all along. We were, after all, working with Fire.

He crouches next to me, stroking my hair; a cool washcloth sits on my forehead. I can't read the look in his eyes, but he seems to be struggling to say something. I wish I knew what.

"Water," he says at last. "Water is the element associated with the west, the setting sun, and thus with death and dying. It is also the element most closely linked to submission and surrender. It stands for emotion, intuition, dreams, visions, and certain forms of healing; it is represented by a chalice or a grail in all the traditions that I know of, including mine." As he bends over to kiss me, I can see from his shaking arms that he, too, is exhausted. "Water is a common symbol for the divine feminine. Open your legs for me. And remember that you are still in the middle of a learning session, and I have not yet given you leave to use your voice."

The couch upholstery scrapes my skin raw as I comply; I wince.

His hand finds the cleft between my legs; he parts my lips with his fingers and covers me with his mouth, and as he laps me gently with his tongue I am lost, trying to remember to not use my voice. Over. And over. I can't stop. I can't scream. My pleasure screams for me, my body convulsing in a rictus of sensation until I sink into the couch, faint and gasping from *petit mors*.

And then he surfaces and plunges himself into me.

"Earth," he says, in the shortest instructional lecture he has ever made, and that is all he says about Earth. But he is obviously near the end of his energy. And that is all he needs to say about Earth, anyway. We both know what Earth is for; we also know what grounding is, and we know what the common ways are to ground power. This is one of the more classic grounding methods.

I tap him lightly on the hand.

"Yes?"

I whisper, barely audibly, "May I..."

"Yes."

And I wrap my legs around his hips and strain with him, moaning with pleasure, and my moans soon become cries, and parched, he covers my mouth with his to drink them in.

We dozed off on the couch for a bit but eventually woke up enough to blow out the candles and relocate ourselves to the bedroom and the futon (one of us limping more than the other) where we lay in a tangle, legs and arms and hair and breath all entwined, kissing each other slowly, languorously.

"One more thing," he says at last. "This is a purely temporary arrangement, as it is a finite apprenticeship; I will therefore not be giving you a collar or any permanent marks of ownership. I only consider those appropriate when there is a lasting commitment. However, I would like you to always wear something of mine while you are under me, some kind of token or favor to remind you of me. That is, if you feel comfortable doing so. I don't want to impose." He strokes my cheek. "Is there anything you might particularly like? You are, after all, the one who is going to be wearing it."

For some reason, this makes me glow as if it were something romantic.

"No, of course I don't mind." I think for a moment. He probably can't afford jewelry on his meager salary. Jewelry has rather serious overtones anyway, even when the jewelry in question is not a ring. Not many options here. "How about a scarf?" I reply at last. "They're discreet enough."

He nods, gets a thoughtful look, then gets up, stumbles to the bureau, and digs around. The scarf he brings out is a large square made of fine black silk. "I'll find something else to put my tarot deck in," he says. "This seems very you; when you asked for a scarf, my tarot cloth came to mind. Black. Of course. I can't think of anything more symbolically appropriate. Give me your right wrist, please."

I hold out my wrist, and he winds the scarf around it, tying it neatly at the ends.

And lies next to me again, and is soon asleep, cradling my wrist and its scarf in his arms. He could almost be a young boy sleeping with a cherished teddy bear.

I look at him and wonder. Eventually, sleep takes me, too.

He drove me home shortly before going to work, dropping me off at my door. I'm used to it now. It took me a little while; I don't like other people to see my apartment, which is a converted attic above a duplex home, and now that it's almost summer, I *really* don't want visitors, because I have no air conditioner, and I can't imagine anyone wanting to stay for even a few minutes in the heat. It's too stifling. I do have a floor fan and a window fan, but they can only do so much.

For one hundred eighty-five per month, you get what you pay for.

If either of my downstairs neighbors moves out, I'm going to take over before the newly vacant apartment even has a chance to be advertised in the classifieds. I don't know what I'll do with that much space, given that both apartments below me are two-bedroom apartments; and I'll have to pay more in rent, of course. Having an apartment with more windows would be nice, though, as would having a kitchen that's equipped with more than just a hot plate, a microwave oven, a toaster oven, and a cube-sized refrigerator. I suppose I'll just have to bite the bullet and look for a roommate.

Another pleasant thing about moving downstairs would be the knowledge that my new dwelling would be legal to inhabit. The reason this attic I'm renting now is so cheap is that it isn't zoned for residence. That's also why the lease is month-by-month, whereas the two regular apartments downstairs have year-long leases.

As I climb the dogleg back stairs from the ground floor to the attic, the heat presses against me, clinging to me until I stagger and have to stop and pant for breath. I'll get used to it in a few minutes. It could be worse. It probably will be worse in a week or two.

I have a few hours to kill until I have to catch the bus. Finally, they transferred me to an evening shift – and the days are long enough that I won't have to walk home in the dark when I get off at my bus stop on the way back. Later in the year, getting home from work is going to be scarier, because I'll have to walk on several blocks of dark side streets, but I'll deal with that when the time comes. It could be worse. The neighborhood I'm in is at least half populated by college students who wanted something within walking distance of the university but couldn't afford student housing. Or at least, that's the case about half a mile or so north. Students don't seem to want to live here on my section of the street. I'm not sure why. It's run-down, and it's noisy on the weekends, but it's not awful. A few blocks away is the street that runs by the county jail. That neighborhood's rougher than this one. No students would ever want to live there, even though it's a little closer to the university than the community here.

On my way to lying down on the mattress I use as my bed, I grab a box of store-brand cornflakes. I'll eat them dry. I have no milk right now, and I won't be able to shop for food until next payday. I make a note to get the toasted oat cereal next time in case I go without milk again. The box of cornflakes is larger, but toasted oats are more filling and easier to eat dry.

I also grab the copy of *Wuthering Heights* that I took out of the library. It's interesting how much more fun it is to read literary classics on my own than it is to read them because I was assigned the book as part of an English class. It's nice to not be compelled. Or maybe I just appreciate my assignments more now that I no longer have access to them. I'm reading the Cliff's Notes to the books, as well. They're the next best thing to a lecture or a discussion, and I'm not even being graded on my work. It's an interesting change of pace from my usual fare of science fiction and fantasy novels.

Especially this one. Catherine and Heathcliff are complete jerks. I can't wait to see what they'll do to each other and their hapless relatives next. The Kate Bush song makes their story sound so very romantic; it lies by omission. These two are not a romantic couple. They're an evening soap opera waiting for a scriptwriter.

When I first moved up here with the girlfriend I was seeing at the time, we signed the lease for this apartment because it was a place that we could get on short notice, without needing a massive deposit. (I had met her through the campus gaming group and the campus Lambda Society, which, like the medieval reenactment club, were also open to townies, including former-students-be-come-townies like me. As it turned out, we had almost nothing in common except gaming and sapphistry; but we were both women, we were both unattached, and we happened). We moved to this city because she had been hired as a grocery store cashier here; she had interviewed for the out-of-town position because she wanted to be closer geographically to her grandmother, who was getting on in years and needed a little help. The only problem with getting employed immediately at a job that is an hour away from where you live is that you have to move right away. So we moved. New jobs, new apartment. And yes, a toaster oven was involved. One can't set up lesbian house without a toaster oven. It is known.

The timing couldn't have been better. After the next-door neighbor caught a brief glimpse of me and my new girlfriend through my apartment window before we pulled down the shade and turned off the lights, he'd taken to standing at his window, directly opposite from the one he saw us through, with a shotgun in his arms. Through the window, he could see that all I had was an efficiency apartment and that there was only one bed: a double mattress, the mattress that we wound up taking up here to the new place when we moved. It had gotten to the point where I was avoiding my own apartment and we were spending almost all our time at hers, just to avoid being shot. It was not at all an easy walk to and from the fast-food restaurant where I worked stocking the salad bar and washing dishes, but at least she didn't have neighbors pointing shotguns at her.

The new job and the new apartment in the new city outlasted the relation-ship. My girlfriend met a man shortly after we settled in here, and that was that.

It happens.

From what I've read, it happens a lot.

Unfortunately, what I've read also says that I am just as likely as my ex to leave a girlfriend for a man the instant a man shows up in my life, because I'm bisexual and therefore not really "womyn-identified," whatever that means, and so I shouldn't be surprised or hurt if my bisexual girlfriend abandons me for a guy, since I'd do the same to her, and really, oughtn't I be looking for couples to date, so that I could be truly satisfied, and not have to inflict myself on proper lesbians when I'm just going to break their hearts with my inherent faithlessness anyway?

Needless to say, I find that advice less than helpful.

The drunks are yelling more loudly, now; I hear the sound of glass shattering. I hope somebody with a telephone line calls the police soon before things get really out of hand.

When we were first settling in, the noises on our block used to keep us awake. Neither my girlfriend nor I had yet grown accustomed to sleeping through yelling, loud music, and other disturbances. We'd been spoiled by living in a small college town on a street that was well away from both the main drag and the college itself. (It took her less time to acclimate to our new surroundings, though than it took me; she had been raised here and was coming back, so none of this was new to her).

One night I had been startled to hear a chainsaw. "It's three in the morning. Isn't it unsafe to chop down trees? Is that even allowed?"

My girlfriend gave me an odd look. "That's not a chainsaw. It's a machine gun."

Oh.

This is why I don't go out much unless it's to catch the bus to work, buy food, or go to the library.

I'm used to it now. Really, I am.

Four more hours until my shift in the call center starts. If I soak one of my tee shirts with water, the evaporation might keep me cool for the time I need to kill. I get up, strip off my clothes, wet down a large tee shirt that I wear when I sleep, and flop back onto my mattress. If I pretend hard enough, the air blowing on me from the floor fan will transform into the wind blowing across the moors. I will enjoy Cathy and Heathcliff behaving badly better if I can sit on the moor to watch them.

ABOUT THE AUTHOR

Sera Maddox Drake – https://seradrake.wixsite.com/seramaddoxdrake – fell to Earth several eons ago and skulked around doing odd jobs (trilobite herding, quantum particle illumination, stromatolite swaddling, mayhem instigation, dragon impersonation, peirazomancy, data entry) until they found an opportunity to write a book. Alternately, they find it both impossible and bizarre to draft an author bio that humble-brags about published writing, literary connections, experience, etc when there is nothing to put on the page, other than "This is my first book. It will be part of a trilogy, and I am self-publishing it, and the two sequels, under a pseudonym."

They live in one of the many rectangle-shaped states in Flyover Country with their spouse, children, and pets.

This bio is much too strange to have been written by a chatbot, but if you need further verification that *Morsels* was written by a living person, the author has an online presence.

Social media to further demonstrate that the author is not a toaster:

Facebook – https://facebook.com/sera.maddox.drake
Goodreads – https://goodreads.com/author/show/47646299.Sera_Maddox_Drake
Wattpad – https://wattpad.com/user/SeraDrake
Instagram – https://instagram.com/seradrakethebookwyrm
Pinterest – https://pinterest.com/SeraDraketheBookwyrm
Medium blog – https://medium.com/@seramaddoxdrake
YouTube – https://www.youtube.com/@SerafinDrake
But don't look on TikTok. The author has a severe nano allergy to pixels and avoids TikTok to avoid triggering their self.

NOBODY IS THIRSTIER THAN A SELF-PUBLISHED DEBUT AU-THOR. If you liked this book, please leave a glowing review on Amazon or Goodreads.

ANCILLA
MASTER, TEACH ME
https://1link.st/seramaddoxdrake
AMO, AMAS, AMAT, AMAMUS, AMATIS, AMANT

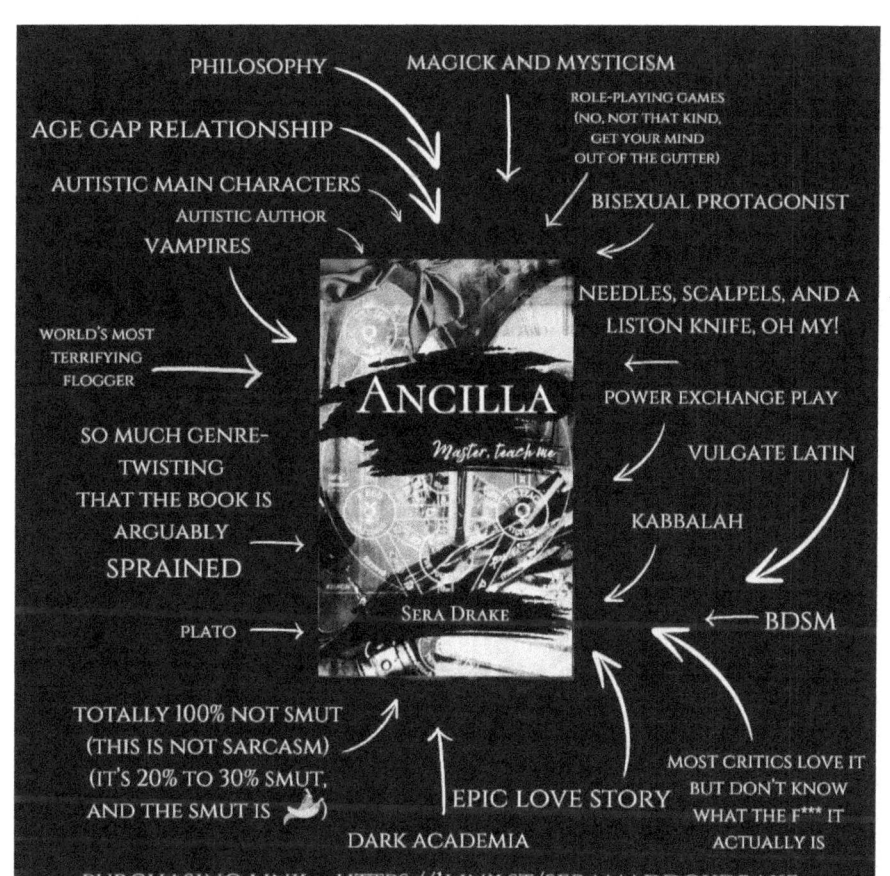

PHILOSOPHY

MAGICK AND MYSTICISM

ROLE-PLAYING GAMES
(NO, NOT THAT KIND,
GET YOUR MIND
OUT OF THE GUTTER)

AGE GAP RELATIONSHIP

AUTISTIC MAIN CHARACTERS

AUTISTIC AUTHOR

BISEXUAL PROTAGONIST

VAMPIRES

WORLD'S MOST
TERRIFYING
FLOGGER

ANCILLA

Master, teach me

NEEDLES, SCALPELS, AND A
LISTON KNIFE, OH MY!

POWER EXCHANGE PLAY

SO MUCH GENRE-
TWISTING
THAT THE BOOK IS
ARGUABLY

SPRAINED

VULGATE LATIN

KABBALAH

SERA DRAKE

PLATO

BDSM

TOTALLY 100% NOT SMUT
(THIS IS NOT SARCASM)
(IT'S 20% TO 30% SMUT,
AND THE SMUT IS 🕊)

EPIC LOVE STORY

MOST CRITICS LOVE IT
BUT DON'T KNOW
WHAT THE F*** IT
ACTUALLY IS

DARK ACADEMIA

PURCHASING LINK - HTTPS://1LINK.ST/SERAMADDOXDRAKE